ABANDONED!

For other titles in the Target Series see end pages

ABANDONED!

The moving story of a kitten abandoned
on wild and lonely Dartmoor

G. D. GRIFFITHS

Illustrated by Les Edwards

First published in Great Britain by World's Work, Ltd., 1973

First published in this edition by Universal-Tandem
Publishing Co., Ltd., 1974

Second impression 1975

Reprinted in 1976 by Tandem Publishing Ltd.

ISBN 0 426 11367 5

Target Books are published by Tandem Publishing Ltd,
14 Gloucester Road, London SW7 4RD
A Howard & Wyndham Company

Printed in Great Britain by litho by The Anchor Press Ltd
and bound by Wm Brendon & Son Ltd
both of Tiptree, Essex

One

The kitten was dozing, curled up head-to-tail on the back seat, when suddenly the car stopped and her mistress, picking her up by the scruff of the neck, carried her to a patch of long grass at the roadside and flung her into it. Her dignity badly ruffled, the indignant kitten was tempted to stay there sulking, then, deciding that it must be some new kind of game, she struggled through the jungle of tall stems in time to see the woman hurry into the car and slam the door.

It seemed an easy enough game to play. The kitten happily made for the vehicle, her pointed tail held high as she bounded along the grass verge, threading her way between tussocks of grass and clumps of nettles. Tripping over a tangle of dead grass, she fell headlong on her nose, and when she had scrambled to her feet again the car was roaring off in a haze of exhaust fumes.

The game was growing difficult to understand, but it was pleasant enough waiting on the sun-warmed grass at the side of the road. Her mistress would be sure to come back soon, laughing at the luxurious way she was stretched out in the sun and picking her up to hug and stroke her until she purred with pleasure.

As time went on and there was no sign of the woman, the kitten began to feel apprehensive and decided to wash, as cats do when they are worried or uncertain. First, each hind leg was stretched out and licked in turn, then both forelegs, paying special attention to the fleshy pads of the feet and the spaces between the toes. Her neck and ears she cleaned with her moistened fore-paws, wrinkling her brows with the effort and darting quick glances round her after every stroke to make sure that no enemy had crept up unheard. She bobbed her head to wash the white bib on her chest until it was damp with spittle, licking the corners of her mouth to ease the ache at the root of her tongue. By then, she felt soothed but too tired to go on with her toilet, so she decided to finish by washing her tail, holding the tip of it between her forepaws and licking and biting it from end to end.

Relaxed and comforted, the kitten curled up and dozed on the grass until the sun sank behind a hill and the chill brought by the lengthening shadows woke her. Frightened and beginning to realise that this was no game, she set off in the direction the car had taken. The road was rough and dusty, little more than a cart-track, and on either side the unfenced moor, broken only by thickets of brambles and an occasional copse, stretched into the distance as far as the eye could see. The kitten padded slowly along in the middle of the road; there was no traffic, and the dust felt soft and warm to her feet.

Night fell suddenly, as it does on Dartmoor, and the eerie hoot of an owl sent the kitten bounding into a clump of heather, where she lay nerve-taut and trembling until the unknown danger had passed. Born in a town, she only knew the sights and sounds of the busy street where she had lived; the only wild creatures she had come in contact with were a few mice and one or two bedraggled house sparrows.

After a while, she summoned up enough courage to go on and stalked along the grass verge, her jet-black body merging into the shadows, only the white of her bib faintly showing. She felt very tired and frightened; only the hope that she would find the car and her mistress round the next bend kept her going. Her paws were grey with dust, and dried goose-grass clung to her flanks and the tail which drooped dispiritedly behind her.

The road began to go steeply downhill; there was a damp, earthy smell and the sound of running water. The grass verge ended in a patch of mud, and the kitten's way was barred by a water-splash, but with her keen night sight she quickly spotted a row of stepping-stones marching across the ford. Daintily stepping on to the first one, she stooped to drink, water which was clear and cold with a strange, peaty taste, but it quenched her thirst and gave her strength to carry on. The last stepping-stone was too far from the bank, and the leap she made across the gap fell short, but she scrambled thigh-deep through mud and water to the bank and plodded on, the mud on her legs slowly caking into hard ridges which pulled painfully on her fur. Still she struggled on, overcoming her exhaustion by sheer will-power. The pads of her feet were sore and blistered, and never in her twelve weeks of life had she felt so frightened and alone. Whenever she had fallen out of the box where she had been born, she had panicked for a moment or two, but her frantic mewing had always brought her mother to seize her by the scruff of the neck and dump her back among the rest of the squirming litter. When her two brothers had gone from the box, carried off in strange arms, she had felt uneasy and alarmed at the time, but she had forgotten them in a day or two.

She wondered why her mistress had behaved so strangely that morning, hugging her tight and stroking her until the man of the house had roughly told the woman to stop it and get into the car. Some frightening things had happened to the kitten since then, but she had never known such anguish of mind or such aching tired-ness as she felt now.

The road began to climb steeply, but the kitten staggered on, panting and near collapse. She sensed that humans were near and that she was leaving the darkness and danger of the moor behind.

At the top of the hill, a hamlet straggled along the road in the moonlight. In the first house, a dog started a frantic barking, sending the kitten scurrying down the deserted road until a sharp bend brought her face to face with a warped wooden gate swinging open on a path hedged with privet. She smelt food not far away.

The path went round the house to the back door, and there she found a saucer of milk and a plate of scraps.

After she had eaten all the food and licked the saucer dry, she sat on the doorstep of the house, wailing her grief to the moon, but her reedy, plaintive cry brought no answer from the sleeping world. Soon, too tired to crawl away to a more comfortable place, she fell asleep on the step.

She was still sleeping on the doorstep next morning when the woman of the house found her and told her husband. They knew the kitten had taken the food and milk they had put out for their pet hedgehogs because the dishes were both licked clean; hedgehogs always leave muddy paw-marks on them.

The man from the house carried the kitten to the top end of the garden, her paws and tail dangling limply from his hands, and dropped her over the fence, still sleeping soundly, into a clump of grass in the lane behind the house. He told his wife that she must not encourage the kitten to stay; they did not want a stray coming to steal the hedgehogs' food.

The kitten slept on, and the sun was riding high in the sky when she awoke with a start. Like all cats, she was instantly in full possession of her faculties and she remembered all the frightening things that had happened to her the day before. Her legs and tail were still thick with dried mud, the blisters on her paws were swollen and tender. Her mouth was parched, so she could not wash herself, and her stomach ached with a gnawing hunger. The milk and scraps she had stolen the night before had not been enough to satisfy her, but she knew where the food had been and she set off to see if she could find some more there.

The back door of the house was closed, and the two

dishes stood empty on the step. The kitten licked the milk-saucer, but it tasted dry and sour. If she stayed on the doorstep, somebody would be sure to come, and it was pleasant sitting there in the sun, easing the aches from her limbs in its warmth, but she grew more and more hungry as she waited. She mewed piteously, but still nobody came to the door, so she began to cry continuously, padding to and fro on the step, unable to believe that food would not be brought out to her.

The door opened with a rush, and the kitten was drenched in the downpour from a bucket of icy-cold water. As she rushed off up the garden path, the man told his wife that that was the best way to stop strays hanging round. There's nothing like cold water to get rid of them; it ruffles their dignity as well as making them feel cold and miserable, he told her.

Unable to believe that one of the humans she still trusted and relied on for food had treated her so cruelly, the kitten spent the afternoon hiding in the rhubarb patch at the top end of the garden. She still expected that the door would open and a friendly voice would call her to eat, but she was too frightened to go near the house until the people who lived there made some move towards her. The water thrown over her had washed some of the mud from her fur, and she was able to ease her parched mouth by licking her damp coat. The shock of being chased off in such an undignified manner had made her forget her hunger for the time being, but she felt more miserable and dispirited than ever. Her fur gradually dried in the warmth of the afternoon sun, and towards evening she felt a little better and slept fitfully for a while.

When night fell, she decided to risk going to the house again. Already, after little more than a day of life as a stray, she was beginning to feel the stirring of unfamiliar emotions; the craft and guile of her forebears were beginning to colour her thoughts, and she did not feel so lost and helpless. She slunk from shadow to shadow along the path, carefully circling the food-dishes before she went to them. They were both empty, and she wrinkled her nose in distaste at their sour, stale smell.

The door of the house was closed, and the kitten sensed instinctively that no food would be brought out to her.

As she went slowly and stealthily round the house and along the front path, she heard a faint rustling and froze, her whiskers twitching, her nostrils wide, her head stretched out. She nosed slowly into the hedge, and there she found a fledgeling blackbird, its beak opening and closing in little soundless cries. It had fallen from the nest earlier in the day, but the hen bird was still keeping watch over it from a branch above. She swooped down on the kitten as she batted the little bird with her fore-paw, and the kitten felt the sudden shock of a sharp beak stabbing at her shoulder muscles, but neither that nor the blackbird's frantically-beating wings could stop her; instinct told her to kill. The fledgeling bird was tender, juicy meat, rich with hot life-blood, and the kitten tore it apart mouthful by mouthful, crunching the soft bones and leaving only the beak and a bit of the spine.

Strengthened by the first food she had tasted for nearly twenty-four hours, she sat on the path washing herself, feeling more and more relaxed with every stroke of her tongue.

Two

The kitten lurked around the garden for several days; she was still domesticated enough to feel happier when she was near humans. She was inexperienced at hunting for herself and found food difficult to obtain; the little blackbird had been easy prey, but she could not manage to catch any other birds, however carefully she stalked them. There were plenty of field-mice in the garden, and the smell of them constantly whetted her appetite, but they evaded her clumsy pounces with contemptuous ease. The people of the house, knowing she was still around, did not put out any food for the hedgehogs, and the kitten grew more and more hungry.

She managed to catch a few flies and a wasp, but the wasp stung her tongue, making it swell so much that she could not even comfort herself by washing. She gnawed a few bones that she found on the compost heap, but she did not find any of these things very appetising and there was little or no nourishment in them. The puddles of rain water on the garden path supplied her with water for drinking, and she spent most of the day curled up in the double hedge which ran along the back lane.

At last, she realised that the people of the house did not want her and that no more food would be put in the dishes on the doorstep. That night, in the dark of the moon, she pushed through a gap in the front hedge of the garden and set out to explore the rest of the hamlet. The sores on her feet were almost healed, but her coat was still tattered and staring, and her bones stuck out under her sagging skin. Her eyes shone green and enormous in her heart-shaped face, catching every gleam of light. She moved slowly and stealthily; the plump, soft kitten, well-fed on three good meals of meat and fish every day, was becoming a creature of the wild, with the instincts of a wild animal, the urge to kill to live and the need to hide when danger threatened. She still had a lingering feeling that her place was with humans, and a vague sense of bewilderment and loss, but with every day that passed she felt more at home in her new life.

The only wild creatures that did not run away from her were the hedgehogs; even the young ones treated her with contempt, scurrying about their business with a flick of their prickly tails. Once she had crept up on one of them when it was rooting for slugs in the strawberry-bed. The urchin froze, watching the slowly-stalking cat with its black and beady eyes, then when she pounced it flipped upwards with its hindquarters, catching the corners of her eyes and her tender nose and lips with its sharp spines. After that, the kitten had left all hedgehogs alone.

The gardens of the houses in the hamlet ran along both sides of the road, and the kitten prowled around each of them in turn looking for food. In one, she found a few hard crusts of bread, thrown out for the birds, and in another there was some gristle, chewed and left by a dog. By then, she was so hungry that she was glad to eat them all.

When dawn broke, she curled up on a pile of empty sacks in a tool-shed in one of the gardens, but the sun had not climbed very high in the sky when there was a swift patter of feet into the shed, then a frenzied, ear-splitting yelping which made her bound in terror on to a shelf stacked with seed-boxes. A mongrel dog, his eyes shining with excitement, his jaws slavering, jumped again and again, trying to grab her tail and drag her down. The kitten felt a strange prickling down her spine, her body arched instinctively and she surprised herself with the vicious spitting sound she made.

The dog's yapping grew more and more frantic, his leaps higher and higher, and the kitten was beginning to wonder how much longer she would be able to stay on her precarious perch among the seed-boxes when she heard a man's voice telling the mongrel to be quiet.

With a last frantic burst of barking, the dog ran off. As soon as she thought it safe, the terrified kitten leapt down from the shelf and dashed madly out of the shed. She did not stop running until she had passed the last house in the hamlet and had once more reached the solitude of the moor.

She spent that day sleeping in a clump of grass and heather, but she was still not confident enough to turn her back on humans entirely, and when dusk fell the sudden hoot of an owl sent her scurrying back in terror to the gardens. The evening was warm and dry, with gnats and mosquitoes gathering in clouds through which bats swooped shrilly, terrifying the kitten as they dived low, angered by her presence in the gardens. Their ear-splitting squeaks set her teeth on edge, and she scurried into the porch of the nearest house, where she was found next morning by the woman who lived there.

The woman was shocked at the state of the kitten. Her eyes and paws looked enormous compared with her emaciated body, and she was very dirty. After the woman had given her some scraps and milk, she sponged the kitten's fur clean and brushed it dry while she purred with pleasure, arching her back and rubbing herself against the woman's hands. Soon the kitten was curled up head to tail, sleeping soundly on some thick pieces of old blanket in a warm box in the kitchen.

She was still asleep when the woman came down next morning. The woman woke her up and put her outside the back door for her morning airing, watching anxiously in case she ran away, but she was pleased to have food and a home again and did not wander far from the house. After a while, the woman opened the door again, and the kitten trotted in, mewing softly with pleasure.

She stayed at the house for nearly a month and became very fond of her new owner. Her coat grew thick and glossy again, her body filled out with plentiful food and milk, and the size of her paws showed that she would be an exceptionally big cat when she was full-grown.

One evening, there was a loud, impatient knock on the door, and the kitten heard the voice of a man. It brought back faint, disturbing memories of the days when she had lived in another house in another, far-away town.

That night, the woman stealthily moved the kitten's box from the kitchen to a spare bedroom, and next day she was fed upstairs and smuggled in and out of the garden for her daily airings. She sensed that something was amiss and tried to explain her worries to her mistress, but the woman took no notice of her anxious mewing.

The kitten did everything she could to show her affection, twining herself between her mistress's legs when she walked and rubbing against her hands when she brought food and milk. She leapt on to the woman's lap when she stooped to put the food down, arching her back and trying to press her head up under her owner's chin, her whole body throbbing with affection and gratitude, but the preoccupied woman brushed her aside.

Worried by the woman's behaviour and afraid that she had offended in some way she did not understand, the kitten anxiously tried to follow her downstairs. Her mistress shooed her back into the room, but the kitten managed to dodge her and ran down to the kitchen, where the woman's husband, home from sea, was sitting. There were loud, angry words between the two humans, then the woman carried the kitten out in her box to the tool-shed in the garden.

She went to the front door, mewing piteously, but the woman carried her back to the shed and gave her some milk and scraps out there. The kitten was anxious and puzzled, and she missed her mistress and the warmth of the kitchen.

Next morning, she padded to the back door of the house, crying in bewilderment, but the man chased her away. Nobody brought food out to her, and after a while she set up a plaintive mewing outside the house. Suddenly, the door was flung open, and the man came out, shouting angrily, but the kitten, realising that he meant danger, scuttled off down the path and headed for the moor.

Panting with fright and exhaustion, she dived into a clump of heather and lay there quivering, unable to understand the strange behaviour of humans. She slept fitfully that night, too frightened to leave the shelter of the heather, but when the sun rose she was so hungry that she forgot her fear. Cautiously, she crept back towards the house, circling the garden shed and slinking along the path to the back doorstep.

She had nearly reached the step when the door was flung open and the woman came out, flapping her apron and shooing the kitten away. When she stopped, hurt and bewildered, the woman picked up a handful of gravel from the path and threw it stinging into her face.

Then the man came hurrying out with a bucket of water and flung it at the kitten. Although most of the water splashed harmlessly on the path, her coat was soaked by flying droplets as she slithered round on the gravel and darted off towards the moor.

All that day, the kitten crouched in the heather watching the house, but nobody came out with food. When dusk fell, she was feeling very miserable, but she brightened up a little after she had gone hunting and managed to catch a young field-mouse which took the edge off her ravenous hunger.

Then, drawn by dim memories of comfort and affection somewhere far away, she set her face to the east and padded off across the moor.

Three

The kitten did not consciously remember her first home with the man and woman who had abandoned her at the roadside, but she felt a strange sense of loss and a compulsion to go on and on to somewhere far across the moor, a place where she would find warmth and comfort, security and a sense of belonging.

She was living entirely as a wild animal, hunting her own food, killing cleanly and quickly as a wild animal does, with none of the needless cruelty of the well-fed, domestic cat, and she travelled as a wild creature travels, obliquely, circuitously. Sometimes, she lingered for several days in a place where birds and small rodents were plentiful. Sometimes her track described a wide circle, and she slept at noon in the spot she had slept in the day before, but slowly, steadily she forged on eastwards. She had lost her fear of the vast expanse of the open moor; for the time being it was her home, and she made her way over it with more and more confidence as the days went by.

When autumn faded into winter, her coat began to grow thicker, making her taut-muscled body look more sturdy than it was. She was by then half-grown, and life on the moor had made her very hardy. The tender pads of her paws had grown hard with travelling over rough ground, and she ploughed her way heedlessly through cotton grass, heather and bracken. She no longer shrank from walking in the rain and she swam fearlessly across the chill moorland streams. A wet coat had become part of life to her, but she still found a dry, warm spot for her daily sleep whenever she could.

Christmas found her near Princetown, that bleak, granite village nearly 1,400 feet above sea-level. The weather was fairly mild, and although the moor was brown and soddon with rain, she was still able to find enough food to keep alive. She decided to stay for a few days in a hedge-bank not far from the grim, grey prison. Each morning, before she went to sleep, she watched the convicts filing out to work on the prison farm and she could not settle down until the last drab figure had vanished over a distant hill. She had already nearly forgotten her life with humans and felt a vague unease when they were near.

Soon after Christmas, a cold wind began to blow from the north east, and at night the heather was harsh with frost. Day after day, the sun could not break through the leaden clouds that darkened the sky. The water in the puddles and ditches turned to ice which burnt the young cat's tongue when she licked it, and the wild creatures she lived on began to grow scarce. The icy, nagging wind penetrated even her thick fur, and as the cold grew more and more bitter, she moved nearer and nearer to the cottages and outbuildings clustering round the prison. For the first time since she had set off on her trek across the moor, she felt afraid with a deep, instinctive fear. She knew that all her hard-won skills, all her agility and all her determination to survive could not save her from the biting cold, and instinct told her that there was even worse to come. For a time, she sheltered from the worst of the weather in a disused rabbit-burrow, only leaving it when hunger and thirst forced her to.

Then the snow began to fall. At first, there were only small flakes fluttering down from the lowering sky, dusting the high hills with white and creeping down the valleys to blur the outlines of the rock-piles and gorse-bushes. The icy wind still whistled through the heather, dislodging tiny avalanches of snow from the steep faces of the tors and clitters. The ground was frozen hard, and in addition to competing with stoats, weasels, foxes, badgers, owls and buzzards for what food there was, the young cat had to use all her cunning to save herself from being eaten by the bigger animals. Slowly, she starved.

With each day that passed, the blanket of white on the moor grew thicker. The cat had difficulty going to and from the rabbit-burrow through the deep drifts, and the inside of it was cold and wet with melted snow and slush. She knew that she must find food and warmth or die.

On a bitter, moonless night when the snow was falling fast, driven by a biting wind so strong that it ruffled her coat and showed the white skin at the roots of the fur, she summoned up the last of her strength and crawled to the stable where the warders' ponies were kept. She crept in through a door that someone had carelessly left ajar and curled up in a pile of hay in a disused loose-box. It was warm and dry in there, and there was a mouth-watering smell of mice which made her stomach turn over with hunger, but she was too weak and tired to hunt them.

The stable smelt safe, in spite of its strangeness and the unfamiliar noises made by the sleeping ponies. The young cat fell into a deep sleep and she was still sleeping soundly when some prisoners came to clean out the stable and see to the ponies the next morning. One of the convicts found her, half-hidden in the hay, and lifted her up by the scruff of the neck, holding her high in the air for the other men to see. The animal slept on, a sleep very near to death.

Seeing that the cat was nearly starving, another prisoner, an old "lifer" who had little hope of ever leaving the moor, asked the warder if he could fetch her some milk. The convict hurried off to the kitchen and came back with a plate of scraps as well as nearly a pint of milk. The young cat had been put back in the hay, where she was still fast asleep, oblivious of the noise of men and ponies round her. When the old man put the plate of scraps beside her, the smell of food awoke her, but she was so weak that her legs gave way under her when she tried to stand up to eat. She mewed faintly and sadly turned her head away from the tempting smell of the scraps she could not reach. The convict saw that she was too weak to feed herself, so he soaked a corner of his handkerchief in the milk, moistening her lips with it and dribbling it into her mouth until he had coaxed her to swallow nearly half of it.

Then she fell asleep again, and the man left her, but at noon, before going for his own meal, he went to the loose-box again. The young cat was still sleeping soundly, curled nose-to-tail in the hay, but she woke at once when he touched her, and he helped her to her feet and gave her the rest of the scraps and milk. She ate most of the food and drank all the milk, purring her gratitude and trying to arch her back under the convict's hand as he stroked her, but the effort was too much for her and she sank down in the hay, exhausted. She slept on for the remainder of the day, waking again in the evening to have some more scraps and milk which her new friend had left for her before he was shut up in his cell for the night.

Next day, the warder told the old prisoner that the cat could stay in the stable, but as soon as she was fit she would have to work for her living keeping down the mice and rats. The convict pointed out her long body, her big paws and her small head, telling the warder that she had all the makings of a good mouser and would soon free the stable of vermin when she had got her strength back.

The moor outside was still deep in snow. The whirling flakes fell day and night without ceasing, blotting the far hills from sight and filling the combes until the whole moor was one vast, smooth plain. The temperature fell sharply at night but rose to a little under freezing-point in the day. The pale January sunshine could not penetrate the leaden clouds which blanketed the sky, and a bitter wind blew steadily from the east. In places, the snow lay in drifts fifty and even sixty feet deep, and the old moormen shook their heads, saying that in all their born days they had never known such weather. The creatures of the wild died in their hundreds, starving to death in their holes and burrows under the snow, and the bigger animals were only able to keep alive by preying on each other. A vixen, too weak to go out and hunt, lay in her earth gnawing at her brush in her aching hunger until the hair and flesh were eaten away to the bone. In the end, she was put out of her misery by a weasel that nosed through the snow to find her and suck the warm, red life-blood from her jugular vein.

Most of the wild ponies had long since made their way to the lowlands from the moor, but a few, too old and weak to make the long trek down, lingered on, scavenging household scraps from the farms and cottages and sleeping in the lee of rock-piles at night, but one by one they grew too weak to stand and sank to their knees and never rose again. Ewes, heavy with young, lay buried deep under the drifts, breathing through blowholes made in the snow by the warmth of their breath, but scores of them died of starvation, and the unborn lambs slowly froze to death in their wombs. Buzzards, owls and other birds fell from the air, frozen to death as they flew, and their bodies lay scattered over the snow; there were not enough of nature's scavengers left alive to clear them away. Even the hardy little brown trout in the moorland streams lay motionless as death in the tiny trickles of water which forced their way downstream under the thick ice.

The bitter cold went on through February and well into March, but by then the young cat was well and strong again. She was still living in the stable, growing plump and sleek on the mice she caught and the milk and scraps the old convict brought for her. The ponies had grown used to her being there and took care not to harm her when she rubbed herself against their fetlocks or darted between their legs chasing mice and rats. She accepted the food and affection of the old prisoner, but she was not entirely at ease with him. Although she was grateful for the food he gave her, she still felt a deep distrust of humans and knew from bitter experience that any stay with them was only likely to be temporary. She often lay on the window-sill of the stable staring out across the moor, the pupils of her eyes contracted to slits in the reflected glare of the snow, then with a swish of her tail she would spring down and pad her way back to the loose-box. She knew that a time would come when she would set off towards the rising sun again, but that time was not yet.

Four

When April came, the weather was still very cold; although it was no longer snowing, the wind blowing steadily from the north kept the temperature hovering near freezing-point, and the moor was still carpeted with white. In the stable-yard, the snow had been cleared by the prisoners, but patches of frozen, grey slush still lingered round its edges.

The cat was nearly a year old, almost full-grown, and the old lifer had been right in saying that she would be a good mouser. The stable was nearly free of mice, and she had killed a few young rats as well. The sight and smell of the unclean rats infuriated her, and she would crouch in the shadows beside the corn-bin for hours on end waiting for one of them to pass. Then she would spring, making a lightning quarter-turn while still in the air, so that she landed four-square on the young rat's back, digging deep with her claws to keep her grip. However frantically the rat rushed to and fro, squealing horribly and shaking itself from side to side, it could not dislodge her. Her teeth would bite deeper and deeper into the back of its neck until its spine snapped with an audible crunch. Although an unusually big cat for her age, she still did not have quite enough weight to deal with the full-grown rats; they were too strong for her and could shake her from their backs with one twitch of their powerful shoulders. More than once, only her speed and agility had saved her from death under their slashing fangs. As it was, she had had two superficial bites on her throat, bites which had turned septic because rats' teeth carry infection from the refuse and offal they mainly feed on. The bites had taken a long while to heal, since the young cat could not reach them to wash them properly. Sometimes, she dreamt of the foul-smelling, hateful rats, and her rage would grow so intense that the twitching of her ears and the furious swishing of her tail would wake her with a start.

Since the snow had been cleared from the stable-yard, the cat sometimes padded across it to the gate, but each time, when she saw that the moor was still thickly blanketed with white, she decided to give up her half-formed plan to resume her trek to the east. The old convict noticed her restlessness and sadly realised that she would probably go as soon as the weather grew warmer. He wondered where she had lived before they had found her in the stable; by her colouring she was not a true wild cat, yet she did not seem to want to settle down with people. He hoped that she would stay; the feel of her warm fur and the soft sound of her purring reminded him of a time long ago when another cat had curled up on his knee in the far-off warmth of home.

Towards the middle of April, the north wind swung round to the west, and suddenly the moor was filled with sunshine and soft, warm airs. Everywhere there was the sound of running water as the snow thawed, and overnight the grey of granite and the brown of heather showed through the fast-disappearing blanket of white. Suddenly, the stable-yard was loud with sparrows, and a lark hung in full song high above the moor.

The young cat grew more and more restless, pacing back and forth across the yard with a peculiar, high-stepping gait. Her ears were pricked as if she was listening for something, and her tail was constantly swishing from side to side. At night, she often went out on to the moor and did not return until day-break.

One night, when the moon was full, she was in the stable, feeling more restless and preoccupied than ever. Even the stealthy rustle of a rat in the loose-box went unheeded by her. Curling up in the hay, she dozed for a while, then she slipped into a fitful, uneasy sleep.

The moon was filling the stable with pools of light and the yard was bright as day when she awoke with a start. Far away, on the other side of the village, a cat was wailing. Another one answered its high-pitched cry, and then the night was made hideous by the blood-chilling music of a cat-chorus as three or four different animals set up an ear-splitting din which rose and fell between long intervals of silence.

The young cat answered once from the window-sill of the stable, and then she was away, streaking across the yard in a peculiar, crouching run. She darted down the street in the bright moonlight, a black shadow flitting among the sleeping houses, and did not stop until she found the other cats out on the moor. Although she approached them with the proper humility and diffidence of a stranger, she was at first greeted with threats and hisses, but after a while the other cats decided to accept her. She sat quiet and proud in the shadows as two yowling, spitting toms fought for her.

The next day, she did not go back to the stable; again she felt the compulsive urge to go on. Everywhere Dartmoor was waking from its winter sleep; new heather shoots were thrusting through the sere brown of the previous year's growth, and green bracken fronds were curling upwards to the sun. The gorse bushes were breaking into bud, and in the hollows beside the streams celandines and primroses clustered. All over the moor, the earth was moist and rich with the promise of new life.

The clouds scudding across the sky on the back of the west wind sent down gentle showers of warm rain which washed the bleakness of winter away with the last traces of ice and snow. The clear spring sunshine soaked through the thin top soil, and everywhere the moorland plants rose to its warmth.

The wild ponies, many of them with foals at foot, came up from the lowlands, and lambs bleated and gambolled among the long-woolled moorland sheep.

Each day was a little warmer than the last as billowy, showery April gave way to the longer, sun-drenched days of May. Each night, the moon rose over the sleeping moor, outlining the jagged tors against the starlit sky. Each morning, the sun rose a little farther north and grew a little stronger, dispersing more quickly the swirling wreaths of mist lingering in the hollows.

The she-cat had crossed the wildest part of the moor, the high ridge of land separating the sources of the Dart and the West Okement. Far to the north of the watershed, High Willays, the highest point of Dartmoor, loomed jagged against the sky, backed by the softer outlines of Yes Tor and Cawsand Beacon, and in between lay the most drab and barren area of the moor, used as a firing-range and avoided as much as possible by both wild creatures and humans.

It was the opening of an artillery barrage that stopped the cat in her tracks. The unbearable booming sent her scurrying back along the bank of the West Dart, and she did not stop until she reached the other side of Rough Tor.

After she had rested for a while and recovered from her fright, she carried on southwards along the side of the river, cautiously making her way through the rushes and cotton grass at the water's edge, pausing from time to time to drink from the cold, peaty stream. There was no shortage of food; there were plenty of voles and birds near the stream, and the cat soon learnt to flip the little brown trout from the water with a forepaw. She slowly went on past Beardown Tor until she came to Wistman's Wood.

The tangled branches of the ancient, twisted oaks,

interlaced overhead with creepers, shut out the day so that the wood is in perpetual, eerie twilight, and the ground below is overgrown with ferns, moss and brambles. The place is dank and wet, with lichen hanging like enormous, grey cobwebs from the boughs of the trees. It is said to be the remains of a great forest which covered Dartmoor long ago, and some moormen believe it to be a former sacred grove of the Druids, still haunted by evil spirits.

It was impossible for the cat to penetrate the dense undergrowth. After trying three or four times to bound over or through it, she gave up and turned eastward again, leaving the wood behind her, and crossed the East Dart just above Dartmeet.

It was nearly three weeks since she had left Princetown, and she felt relaxed and happy as she slowly carried on across the moor. She no longer felt the compulsive urge to go on and on, nor did she hanker after the lost comfort of life with humans; she had grown to look on Dartmoor as her home.

In June, about nine weeks after leaving the prison stable, the she-cat began to feel a strange restlessness. From time to time, she stamped out a nest in the heather, but she left each in turn and slowly carried on across the moor. She had lost all desire to hunt and she padded on and on, looking round her uncertainly, until she came to a ruined Bronze Age hut-circle. She found a thick pile of bracken among a jumble of fallen stones inside the tumbledown walls and stretched out on it, panting. She did not know what was happening to her; she only knew instinctively that she had to find somewhere dry and warm and safe.

Her kittens, one male and one female, were born later that day, and as she washed their damp, squirming little bodies, she was happier than she had ever been in all her short life. A fierce desire to cherish and protect them swept over her, and she curled her body round them, purring her pleasure.

Five

The cat did not leave her litter until the pale streaks of light in the eastern sky showed that dawn was near. Then, weak from her labour and aching with hunger, she cautiously crawled from the nest of bracken. Out on the moor, she pounced on a young rabbit playing in the dew-soaked heather and tore savagely at its still-living flesh. Soon her fierce hunger was gone.

After she had left the nest, her two kittens squirmed around in their sleep, missing the warmth and reassurance of their mother's body. They crawled close together, each with its head pillowed on the flank of the other, trying to keep warm, but they were beginning to shiver in the morning chill when the she-cat came back. All that day, the kittens slept and suckled, and their mother lay curled round them, talking to them in deep, throaty undertones and washing them carefully after each feed, her eyes shining with pride and pleasure.

As evening drew near, she began to grow restless; her sharp ears had caught the faint sounds of stealthy movement outside the hut-circle, and her nose twitched as it picked up the scent of a fox. The bed of bracken among the tumbled stones was difficult for any but a small animal to reach, so there was little danger to the kittens from the fox. Even so, the cat was very worried about her young; already they were able to make little mewing sounds, and she realised that some smaller animal, such as a stoat or a weasel, might hear the noises the kittens made and kill them while she was out looking for food, unable to protect them.

As the night went on, she grew more and more restless, torn between her hunger and her fear for her young. She stood up and looked out of the nest. The whole of the moor was bathed in brilliant moonlight, and every leaf and stone stood out as plainly as if it were day. Inside the ruined hut-circle, nothing stirred. The cat listened intently; far away across the moor, a lamb bleated and a ewe answered it; from down a nearby valley came the murmur of running water. The fox was gone, and the she-cat could neither see nor smell any other danger.

She left the hut-circle and padded on until she came to a pile of rocks, heaped together in a sort of cairn, with a number of cave-like holes among the bigger stones at the base of the pile. She explored each hole in turn; they all smelt warm and dry, but they were too easy to get at for her liking. About half-way up the cairn, a displaced lump of granite left open the downward-sloping way to a roomy chamber, snug and dry and thickly-floored with wind-blown leaves. The entrance was narrow and well-hidden and high above the ground. The cat knew at once that it was a perfect home for her and her litter.

On her way back to the nest, she killed and ate a field-mouse which took the edge off her raging hunger. She heard faint rustlings in the dense shadows at the feet of other rock-piles that she passed and knew that more mice were there for the taking, but she had more urgent work to do. The bright moonlight made her anxious; the sleeping moor spread out so clearly before her seemed full of dangers, and she could not rest until she had moved her family from the hut-circle.

The kittens were fast asleep, curled head-to-tail, when the she-cat returned to the nest. She took the young tom first, lifting him up in her teeth by the scruff of the neck and carrying the limp little body carefully to their new home in the rock-pile. The lumps of granite were hard to climb with her dangling burden, but she eased her way up them one by one until she was able to back into the new nest and gently lay the kitten down on the thick bed of dried leaves. She nudged him into the centre of the nest with her nose, then she hurried off to fetch the she-kitten, and soon both her young were contentedly sleeping in the circle of her body. The strangeness of their new quarters did not worry the kittens; to them, their mother and the comfort she gave them meant home and safety.

The two kittens grew quickly. On the ninth day, their eyes were open, and from then on they grew more and more active. The little tom was black, with white paws and a white bib, the she-kitten was a tortoiseshell and they both had bright blue eyes. They were full of mischief, and although the upward slope of the nest stopped them falling out when they played together, their mother always lay across the entrance when she was with them, blocking it with her body to make sure they came to no harm. The youngsters pawed and batted at each other, and when they tired of that they tumbled and rolled and tussled all over the floor of the nest. Sometimes their mother lost patience with them and cuffed them soundly for some piece of mischief. She kept them spotless; when they did not want to be washed and struggled to get away from her, she held each down in turn with her paw across its body until she decided it was clean enough to be let go. If she was annoyed with the kittens, she was quite rough when she cleaned their eyes and ears with her tongue, but she forgot all their trying ways when she suckled them. She lay relaxed, with her eyes shut, purring with deep contentment as they nestled close to her body.

Soon the youngsters were old enough to be carried out of the nest to play in the sunshine among the stones at the foot of the cairn. Their mother always stayed near, washing herself and sometimes dozing lightly in the sun, but all the time she was on the alert for any danger to her young.

The she-cat, like all cats, was a good mother and trained the two kittens thoroughly. She taught them to be clean, to run to her when she mewed, to freeze when she told them to and above all to move silently and stealthily. In their play, they taught themselves how to hunt; to crouch with tail stretched out and then to pounce with unsheathed claws, sinking their teeth in the neck of their make-believe prey and using their weight to bear it to the ground.

As they grew older and more confident, their mother started to take them out hunting with her and, as the first step towards weaning them, taught them how to suck the flesh and lap the blood of the birds and animals she caught.

It was a long, dry summer; the sun blazed down day after day from a clear blue sky, and even the nights were hot and oppressive. By the middle of August, the moor was an arid waste. The bogs that fed the streams had shrunk and dried; the rivers themselves were mere trickles winding their slow and tortuous course over the clearly-visible quartz pebbles of their beds. Sheep, cattle and ponies came from all over the moor to graze on the coarse grass at the edges of the streams; the sap had dried out of the heather, the bracken was sere and lifeless long before its season. During the day, a purple heat-haze hung shimmering over the granite tors, and at night the stone radiated heat like an oven. The few trees that had managed to grow on the high moors by taking root in earth-filled crevices in the granite had already shed their leaves, and there were neither hips on the briar roses nor haws on the thorn trees.

The kittens and their mother had left their old home in the rock-pile and moved westwards to live beside one of the rivers, where they had made a nest in a hollow tree on the bank. The drought provided them with plenty of food; many of the smaller animals staggered down to the shrunken river so weakened by lack of water that they had lost all sense of caution. Mice, voles, squirrels and rabbits made their way along the dried-up tributaries, scenting the water they desperately needed in the main stream and falling easy prey to all the predators, who grew sleek and fat on their victims' flesh and blood.

By the beginning of September, the two kittens were weaned, and although they still relied on their mother's superior strength and cunning for most of their food, they killed quite a number of thirst-weakened small animals and birds themselves. They grew strong, lusty, sleek and well-fleshed like their mother.

Later in the month, some people camping on the moor for the night left a bottle lying in the heather when they moved on. Next morning, the rays of the sun, magnified by the glass, set the tinder-dry under-growth smouldering until a light northerly breeze sprang up and fanned it into flames which ran through the parched heather with lightning speed. In a few hours, what had started as a tiny, smouldering spark had grown into a blazing inferno raging over a large area of the moor. Driven by the breeze, it sped on southwards, leaving behind it a blackened, reeking waste where nothing stirred. The sunset was blotted out by a purple cloud, and when the moon rose, its pale light was lost in the dark pall of smoke hanging over the moor.

The she-cat had been uneasy all day and had several times left the hollow tree where she and the kittens were sleeping to pad restlessly to and fro along the river bank. She did not recognise the strange, disturbing smell which stung and tingled in her nostrils, but she knew instinctively that it meant danger to her and her young. When dusk fell, she took no notice of the kittens when they tried to lead her northwards to the family's usual hunting-grounds. She determinedly headed south, and after a while the kittens followed her, mewing their protests.

The she-cat stalked quickly and purposefully along the shingle at the side of the shrunken river, keeping close to the water, bounding across exposed tree-roots, scrambling over rocks, and the youngsters had difficulty in keeping up with her. Sometimes, where the water was shallow, she waded through it to cut a corner, and where the river was deep she swam across, taking the kittens with her one by one, her teeth holding them firmly by the scruff of the neck.

Dawn had broken before she decided that it was safe to stop to rest and drink deeply of the peaty water. By then, they were miles away from the fire, and the breeze, which had veered south during the night, brought on it the clean, fresh smell of the sea. The she-cat snuffed the air and knew that they were safe.

All that day, they slept. The kittens lay side by side with outstretched paws, and their mother slept curled against them, waking from time to time to stretch and yawn and eye the undergrowth on the bank above for possible enemies.

Blown back on itself by the southerly breeze, the fire on the moor had died down while the cat and her litter were sleeping, but at sunset the breeze backed north again and freshened, blowing scattered patches of smouldering embers on to the unburned moorland. Fanned by the wind, they set the parched, sapless heather ablaze in several places. The flames swept southwards, gathering strength as they went, leaping from gorse bush to gorse bush, devouring shrubs, bracken and heather, leaving a charred, smoking wake behind them.

The she-cat woke with a start to the smell of burning and roughly butted the kittens to their feet, still weak, tired and sticky-eyed. She washed their faces with quick, rough strokes of her tongue and spoke to them urgently, telling them to wake up at once. Her agitation communicated itself to the youngsters, who panicked and scampered off in different directions.

By the time their mother had rounded them up, the fringe of the blaze had reached the top of the river valley, and a tongue of fire flickered along each bank with the speed of light. Above the crackling of the rapidly-advancing flames, a deeper and more menacing sound could be heard, the sullen roar of the main body of the fire. Small animals poured out of the smoke and rushed in headlong panic to the river, where some drowned in its deep pools and others died more horribly, burned to death on its banks as the flames leapt and roared over them.

The she-cat pushed the two kittens into a deep pool in the widest part of the river and nosed them towards a flat-topped boulder awash in an eddy near the middle. The young tom, terrified by the falling sparks and the heat and crackle of the flames, swam past the rock and headed for the opposite bank. His frantic scrabblings took him into the main current and he was whirled away downstream, his black head disappearing from sight in the red-tinged, swirling water. The distraught she-cat would have tried to save him, but the tortoise-shell kitten had panicked, too. She had swum off in the opposite direction and was clambering across the shingle and rocks of the shore they had just left. Her mother swam over and bounded up the beach after her, but a gnarled old hawthorn came crashing down from the bank above with one of its glowing branches across the kitten's back. For a few seconds, the tortoiseshell writhed and screamed in agony as her fur blazed up, then she vanished from sight in a shower of sparks from the burning tree.

The cat swam back to the boulder in the pool, where she lay among the drifting sparks, shocked and terrified, until the fire had swept on and the moon had risen over the blackened, lifeless moor.

Then she slowly swam across to the far bank of the river and instantly fell into a deep sleep on a cool, damp patch of shingle at the water's edge.

Six

By dawn, the fire had burned itself out, but wisps of smoke were still rising from the vast expanse of blackened moorland. The cat did not stray far from the cool, damp shingle beside the river that day; she still thought her kittens were somewhere near and called them to her from time to time. She did not hunt; she had no desire for food, but she often drank deeply of the brown, smoke-tasting water to slake her raging thirst. She could not understand that her kittens had gone for ever until she swam to the opposite bank of the river, where she sniffed at the charred body of the little tortoiseshell and licked its one unburned fore-paw. The thing in the ashes neither smelt nor tasted like her kitten, and she lay beside it for a long time, crying pitifully.

When dusk fell, the she-cat decided to go as far away from the smouldering, reeking moor as she could. She travelled south all night, pausing only to drink, making no attempt to prey on the mice and voles that had survived the blaze. The scorched, smoking wilderness left by the fire stretched far into the foothills of the moor, forcing her to keep to the shingle at the side of the river; the bank above was still too hot to walk on. Even so, she sometimes had to wade or swim to avoid the small patches of hot ash which still smouldered near the water's edge, but she went on and on, driven by her fear of the reeking waste which lay around her. Each time she plunged into the river, its waters washed bits of scorched flesh from her flanks and back, but she hardly felt the pain.

At first light, she was trudging across a tract of rough land at the side of the river, and all around her she saw hillocks of strange, grey earth, spoil from the clay-workings there. The air smelt fresh and free of smoke at last, and the blind fear which had driven her downriver from the devastated moor went from her. She left the sandy edge of the river and scrambled up on to the bank, where she crawled into a patch of long grass and fell into a deep sleep.

The sun suddenly shot into the grey-blue morning sky, and with its rising the wild creatures began to stir on the tract of waste land where the she-cat was sleeping. Foxes slunk back to their earths, badgers blundered to their setts, hedgehogs curled up in patches of grass and fallen leaves, moles scurried into the darkness and safety of their underground runs. A sleepy squirrel shook himself awake in the branches of a hazel tree, an otter rolled in the river and a jay flew squawking from an alder.

The cat slept all that day in the patch of grass, lying on her side as if dead, her legs together and stretched out. She did not hear the clank and scrape of the machinery in the clay-pit, and she was still asleep when the hoot of the siren ended the men's work at five o'clock. She was oblivious of the grass snake which slithered past the clump of grass where she lay and the buzzard which hovered overhead, scanning the waste land for prey. The sun gradually dried her wet fur, matted with mud and tangled with burrs, but its warmth was not enough to stem the deadly chill which was spreading through her blood. As the sun travelled slowly westwards, she sank deeper and deeper into the sleep of exhaustion whose only end is death.

When the clay-workers had gone home to their cottages down the valley and silence had fallen on the waste, the watchman took over for the night. After he had lit the brazier outside his little corrugated iron hut, he made his rounds, seeing that the dumpers and all the other equipment and machinery were safe. Then he sat down in the hut and started his first pipe of the night, puffing contentedly as he stared through the open door into the glowing heart of the brazier.

When dusk fell, the man decided it was time to eat some of the sandwiches he had brought with him. There was plenty of tea and milk and sugar on the shelf in the hut, but the bucket in which drinking-water was kept stood empty in the corner.

By then, it was dark outside the hut. Like many country people, the watchman was superstitious and did not like being on Dartmoor at night, and the tract of rough, wild wasteland beside the river was very like the moor. In the hut, with the bright light of a hurricane lamp as well as the glowing brazier just outside the open door, he felt snug and happy. He felt safe enough among the buildings and machinery of the clay-workings, too, but who could say what lurked in the darkness among the reeds and sedges bordering the brown, peaty water of the river, water that came straight down from the moor?

But sandwiches without a cheering can of tea were unthinkable. He picked up the bucket and resolutely set off for the river.

On the river bank, all was still, but just as the watchman was about to go down to the water's edge and fill his bucket, the moon suddenly came out from behind a cloud, and its cold, clear light threw everything into sharp relief. The jagged mass of the high moors hung menacingly over the valley, and in the eerie light the silver-grey sedges along the river bank seemed full of unutterable evil.

The man hurried down to the water and half-filled the bucket, clambering back up the bank with frantic haste. He blundered through a patch of coarse grass and nearly stumbled over something, something that looked very like a cat. As he stared at it, wondering if he was imagining things, the animal's flanks heaved and a faint sigh came from its lips.

Reassured that the cat was flesh and blood, the man's alarm turned to pity; he could see that she was in great distress, perhaps dying. He thought of his own cat, snug and safe in the cottage down the valley, and he took off his jacket to use as a sling to carry the sleeping animal to the hut.

In the hut, he examined the cat carefully and found that, although she was covered with mud and had some superficial burns, she did not seem to be seriously injured. He could find no signs of broken bones, and her limp body was well-covered with flesh. The man wrapped her in a dry sack and sat with her on his lap near the glowing warmth of the brazier, squeezing a few drops of milk between her slack lips from time to time.

Gradually, the cat's breathing grew steadier, and some tension came back to her limbs. She was still sleeping deeply, but it was the healing sleep of returning life, not the coma of approaching death.

When it was time for him to finish work, the watch-man carried the cat to a warm spot in the corner of his hut and made her as comfortable as he could on an old sack, pouring the last of the milk into a saucer and putting it on the floor beside her.

He came back that evening and found the milk still untouched and the cat lying on the sack just as he had left her, but she was sleeping less deeply and her breathing was easier. She purred faintly when he stroked her, and later she awoke and drank a small amount of milk. The man had brought with him a pair of scissors to cut the fur away from her burns, some butter to clean them and to soften the scorched and swollen pads of her feet, some milk and some canned fish.

He tended the cat's burns and cleaned her coat as best he could, and she showed her gratitude by purring softly and trying to rub herself against him, but she was too unsteady on her feet. She ate the fish daintily, paus-ing between each mouthful to look up at the man, thanking him with her eyes, and she drank a whole saucer of milk.

When the watchman went home in the morning, the cat was much stronger, and although her feet were still sore and swollen, she was able to limp round inside the hut.

That evening, the man found the hut empty, and some milk he had left in the saucer was gone, but as soon as he lit his pipe and brewed his first can of tea, the cat slowly padded into the hut, mewing softly. He fed and petted her, noticing that her burns were clean and already showing signs of healing. She stayed with him most of the night, but when dawn broke she went off to sleep in the patch of grass on the river bank where the man had found her.

As the days went by, the cat gradually regained her health and strength. Fur grew again over the scars left by the burns, but it was white, so in addition to her white bib, she had small patches of white on her back and flanks. She spent most of each night with the watchman, sitting in the hut with him or following him like a dog when he made his rounds, but she still went off to sleep in the long grass by the river every day.

Slowly, the golden autumn faded into winter. Each day, the sun gave a little less warmth, and each night was a little colder. The mist hanging over the wasteland in the mornings grew thicker and took longer to disperse, and sometimes the clay-workings were hidden all day in a thick, grey cloud through which the shouts of men and the clank and grind of machinery echoed eerily. The sedges on the river bank were dry and brown, the tangled branches of a hawthorn tree, stripped of its scarlet fruit by birds, hung grey and lifeless over the water.

In a copse at the top end of the waste, the leaves shed by the hazel trees lay in yellowing drifts among the clustered trunks. Patches of nettles seemed to vanish overnight, and the tangled islands of brambles glowed red-brown and lifeless.

One night in December, the watchman knew from the way the flames of the brazier danced and crackled that the temperature was below freezing-point and he retreated further into the shelter of the hut.

When dawn broke, he saw that the edges of an old, flooded clay-pit were fringed with ice, and his breath rose in white spirals in the frosty air. Crows were fluttering, cawing, from the copse, and a young rabbit slowly hopped through the crackling, frost-whitened grass to its burrow in a clump of brambles. The man wondered how the cat was faring in the wintry weather. She had not been to the hut for some time, and he thought that the cold must have driven her to find a home somewhere warmer than the waste. Before he set off for his cottage down the valley, he paused to look up at the moor. The hills were already capped with snow, and the man shivered in the biting wind blowing down the valley from their barren, icy slopes.

By Christmas, the snow-line had crept down to the foothills. Flurries of hail and sleet began to sweep across the wasteland, and the men at the clay-pit went about their work with sacks round their shoulders to protect them from the worst of the weather. The watchman took his brazier inside the hut, where part of the floor was covered with sheet-iron for it to stand on in very cold weather, leaving the window open a couple of inches to let the fumes out. He had not seen the cat for more than a month, although he had seen a dark shape that looked like her, slinking along the river bank.

The new year came in cold and dry. For a few days, the pale sun, shining from an ice-blue sky, gave an illusion of warmth, then suddenly winter struck. The temperature plummetted down overnight, and snow began to fall heavily. In a few hours, the waste was carpeted with white, and the watchman's hut was almost hidden in a drift which covered the shed where the dumpers were kept and stretched nearly to the hazel copse. The snow stopped at dawn, but the heavy, yellow-grey clouds lowering over the moor threatened more to come. The watchman emptied the coke from the brazier, fastened the door of the hut and started to struggle home down the valley, sometimes ploughing through drifts that came up to his armpits.

Later that day, a blizzard driven by a howling north wind hit the foothills of the moor, making it impossible to dig the clay, and all the men were told to go home until they were sent for. For nearly three weeks, the clay-workings and the whole of the upper part of the river valley lay still and silent under a thick blanket of white, then suddenly a warm westerly wind brought the thaw. The snow vanished as quickly as it had come, and the men went back to work again, plodding up the valley along the bank of the swollen river.

When the watchman went to start work, he found that the door of his hut had been torn off its hinges by the wind. Inside, the cat was fast asleep on her old bed of sacking in the corner, and the floor around her was littered with the tails of mice and rats.

Seven

Spring came early, as it sometimes does on the outskirts of the moor. The coarse, green leaves of the winter heliotrope were thick with pungently-scented, pale lilac blossom, and along the edges of the copse snow-drops clustered white among the green spikes of their leaves. The hazels in the copse were covered with danc-ing golden catkins, and clumps of primroses nestled under the trees. The river, swollen by rain and melted snow from the moor, ran high and smooth between its banks, its brown waters spilling over on to the wasteland here and there. When the floods receded, they left on the waste patches of rich alluvial mud from which plants and flowers sprang in their hundreds. Everywhere was moist and full of new life, the earth warm and fertile under the spring sunshine and the mild west wind.

The watchman saw that the cat was growing restless, constantly wandering in and out of the hut, hardly staying long enough even to drink the milk he put down for her before she padded out again. She seemed impatient when the man petted her, but at times she had sudden fits of affection when she would wind herself around his legs, almost tripping him up, purring loudly and sucking at the turn-ups of his trousers. Often she stood outside the hut staring into the night, uttering strange, high-pitched cries, then she would slink off into the undergrowth, still calling.

One night, she went to the hut with a battered, lop-eared, black tom and tried to coax him to go inside with her, but he would go no further than the edge of the circle of light thrown by the brazier, sitting there with his tail twitching, eyeing the man suspiciously. After she had gone into the hut alone and lapped up her milk, the she-cat ran off with him into the darkness. The man wondered where she had found her mate and decided that the tom must have run away from one of the cottages down the valley to live semi-wild on the moor.

The watchman did not see the she-cat for some time, but she turned up again in the middle of May, bringing three coal-black kittens with her. The man was smoking in his hut, looking out through the open door, when he saw eight separate points of light glowing green in the shadows beyond the flickering gleam of the brazier. Two of them moved slowly nearer until the white of the she-cat's bib showed in the red glow of the fire. Behind her, at a lower level, three other pairs of eyes shone emerald as she stopped to coax her kittens to go with her to the hut.

The kittens were very nervous of the man at first, but their mother's attitude towards him told them that no harm would come to them. The she-cat let him pick up each of the kittens in turn to fondle them, but she looked very relieved when he put them down again on the ground beside her. One of the youngsters blundered into a saucer of milk which the watchman had hurriedly poured out, and its mother cuffed it with her paw before starting to wash it. While she was cleaning the clumsy kitten, the other two went over to the saucer and sniffed at the spilled milk, but it went up their nostrils and made them sneeze. Their mother washed them, too, before she lapped up the milk left in the saucer, keeping an eye on her family while she drank.

After she had finished drinking, the she-cat leisurely set about her own toilet, pausing with one hind leg held at right angles to call back one of the kittens when it strayed off into the darkness. Then, groomed and fed, she rounded up her family and led them away on to the waste.

The kittens grew quickly, and all through that summer they regularly went to the hut to see the watchman, sometimes with their mother and sometimes by themselves, but when autumn came all three of them disappeared. By then, they were old enough to hunt their own food, and, having never lived in a house, they were even less dependent on humans than their mother was, so there was little reason for them to stay on the wasteland. The man thought they would come back in time, but in the end he decided that they must have gone away to lead their own lives further up the valley, perhaps on the moor itself. Their mother remained on the waste, sometimes sleeping in the grass beside the river and sometimes in the watchman's hut.

It was a mild winter, with hardly any frost, and January was soft and damp, but in February torrents of rain began to lash down. The moorland bogs absorbed the downpour for a time, but eventually they reached saturation point and began to overflow. Water poured down every ditch and gully, swelling the streams which fed the rivers until the valleys leading from the moor were filled with swirling, brown torrents. The river going through the waste ran full and high, sweeping along with it scores of sheep, rats, rabbits and other animals that had met their death in its rushing waters. The men at the clay-workings toiled day and night building up its banks, bumping and bouncing across the rough land with dumpers full of clay-spoil as fast as the bulldozers could load them.

Then, after three days and nights, the rain stopped and the river gradually began to fall, but late on the fourth night a thunderstorm broke over Cranmere, the great bog in the middle of the moor. The hissing rain poured off the already-sodden land like a tidal wave, sweeping everything before it as it surged down the river valley. The watchman heard a crack like a giant whip, followed by a tumultuous roar which grew louder every moment, and he knew that the river had burst its banks higher up the valley. He ran towards a tall spoil-heap, but before he could reach it a wall of foaming water, carrying gorse bushes, brambles, trees and drowned animals before it, knocked him off his feet and swept him down to the sea.

The swirling flood poured into the clay-pits, covering the bulldozers, scrapers and dumpers in them with nearly two hundred feet of water. The broken pieces of the watchman's hut were whirled away in the seething tide, and his brazier died with a hiss and a spurt of steam before it went rolling down the valley beneath the racing water.

The cat was hunting in the hazel copse when her sharp ears picked up the distant rumble of the approaching flood. Disturbed and alarmed by the unfamiliar sound, she scrambled up a tree and was clinging to one of its branches when the roaring torrent poured through the copse, uprooting everything in its path. Soaked and terrified but still clinging to the tree, she was carried across the waste until the hazel lodged in a clutter of debris swirling round and round in an eddy over what had been one of the clay-pits. The main flood swept on, leaving the expanse of water behind it strangely calm, and the tree the cat was on gradually stopped spinning round to bob gently across the newly-made lake, collecting twigs, leaves, gorse bushes, trees and baulks of timber as it went.

Slowly, the level of the water on the wasteland went down until at dawn the cat was able to swim to the top of a hillock of clay-spoil, where she sat shivering with a toad and a half-drowned squirrel that had already taken refuge there. Neither of them showed any fear of the cat, and she made no attempt to harm them. The pale February sunshine slowly dried her fur, and though she felt no hunger, she quenched her thirst by lapping a little of the brown flood water from time to time.

By the next morning, most of the water had drained

off the waste; only the clay-pits were still full. As soon as the new day broke, the cat set off across the wasteland, bounding from one half-dry spot to the next, her paws and legs plastered with the slimy, grey clay. She knew that she must move to higher ground, so she followed a course which would take her to the foothills of the moor. As she went higher up the valley, the going grew less difficult; the topsoil had been scoured away by the flood, and the clean, hard granite was much easier to travel over than the sticky mud of the lowlands. Several times, she came across mice and voles that had survived the flood. They seemed dazed with fright, making no attempt to avoid her when she pounced on them, and soon her savage hunger was satisfied.

By nightfall, she had reached the outskirts of the moor. Up there, very little damage had been done by the storm. The brown heather roots were wet and rotting, and here and there an uprooted gorse bush marked the track of the rushing water, but the main fury of the flood had hit the river valleys, where its waters had been channelled by the banks of the rivers. Well-fed and tired, the cat looked around for somewhere to sleep and decided on a shelf of rock half way up one of the clitters, high above any possible danger from floods.

The next day dawned bright and warm. It was as if the storm had washed winter away, and the clear moorland air smelt sharp and sweet with spring. Day by day, the sun grew stronger, and a warm west wind chased high, fleecy clouds across the bright blue sky. The drab winter colours and austere outlines of the moor softened as new shoots of heather and bracken sprang up on the slopes of the hills, and here and there a gorse bush burst into a blaze of early bloom. The racing clouds traced rippling patterns over the heather, patterns which broke and re-formed in varying shades of purple, and the strange, ringing silence of the moor was broken again by the song of birds.

The cat travelled north and east, going first in one direction, then in the other, driven on by the urge to climb higher and higher from the flooded river valley. When she came to the main road threading its way across Dartmoor, the sound of the cars going along it filled her with restlessness and mistrust. A dim, disturbing half-memory struggled to find its way into her consciousness, and she lay in a dry ditch for the whole of one day watching them speed by, unable to understand what was making her so uneasy.

When night fell, the cat decided to go on and scuttled across the road during a lull in the traffic. She was ravenously hungry and fed on a young rabbit that she pounced on as he turned to hop off in panic to his burrow. As she carried on across the moor, the cat came to a small village and made a detour to avoid it, but a dog from it picked up her scent and ran yelping after her. She turned to face him, and her arched back, her blazing eyes and the vicious spitting sound she made brought him to a slithering halt. She stalked towards him, stiff-legged and snarling, but the dog slunk back towards the village, barking his defiance when he thought he was at a safe distance.

After that, the cat kept well away from houses and spent the rest of the summer on the open moor, alone but contented. She bore no kittens that year, and when autumn came she was in fine condition. Her winter coat was thick and glossy, so close that, even when the strongest wind ruffled it, no flesh showed at its roots. She was in her prime, a mature and beautiful animal, lithe and strong, stalking free across the uplands of the moor with the stealth, the speed and the grace of the essentially wild creature that she was.

Eight

That summer, one of the lowland farmers had taken his bees to a clearing in the upper valley of one of the south-flowing rivers so that they could gather pollen on the moor and make rich, dark, heather honey.

When autumn came and he went to take them back to the farm, he found one hive empty and damaged, blundered into by a red deer going down to the river to drink. He ruefully decided that the broken hive was not worth taking back home and left it leaning against one of the sycamore trees bordering the clearing.

Sensing that winter was near, the cat had left the high moors and was on her way down to the warmer low-lands when she came to the clearing and was attracted to the damaged bee-hive by the faint, sweet smell of honey.

She decided to stay in the hive for the winter; it was an ideal home for her. The inside was warm and dry, the floor was well above ground level, the roof was still watertight, and the hive was almost hidden under a deep drift of dried leaves to keep it snug and warm. It was near, but not too near, water; it was dry and roomy, yet it was small enough to be kept warm by the heat of her body.

There was plenty of food round about; the river was full of fish, and rabbits, squirrels, voles and mice lived on its banks. The cat began to put on flesh, giving her the weight to bring down larger animals, such as full-grown rabbits. She grew more confident and aggressive, hunting with a ruthless savagery she had never shown before, often killing wantonly when she had no need of food.

One day, she was lying crouched on a low bough overhanging the river bank when out of the corner of her eye she caught a flash of movement higher upstream. As she watched intently, a sinuous, dark-furred animal came weaving its way through the undergrowth along the river bank, stopping now and then to peer into the water. The cat had never seen anything like it; it reminded her of a stoat or a weasel, but its colouring was different, its tail was more bushy, its smell much stronger.

The mink had escaped from a fur-farm down the valley and had been living beside one of the tributaries of the river, but he had wiped out the fish there and was looking for a new hunting-place. He saw the cat perched on the branch but determinedly came on; he was hungry and could see three or four trout rising near her. The cat was still watching the mink carefully as he made his sinuous way along the side of the river. His rank smell revolted her, and his broad, flat head, darting like a snake through the undergrowth, filled her with savage hatred. Her tail twitched slowly, and she poised herself to spring.

The mink gave her one contemptuous glance and stopped under the bough to stare into the water. Mad with rage, the cat pounced on him, landing with all four feet on his lithe body and sinking her teeth in the back of his neck, but with one lightning movement the mink broke free, and his needle-sharp teeth bit into the cat's flank. Screaming with rage and pain, she shook him off and slashed down with her teeth, sinking them into his throat. She could feel her chest and stomach being raked by her opponent's claws, but her thick fur saved her from injury. The body under her frantically flung itself from side to side, but the cat's weight was too much for it. She kept her hold, driving her teeth deeper and deeper through fur and muscle until the mink's jugular vein was torn out. Even with the life-blood spurting from his mangled throat, the mink still fought on, clawing viciously at his adversary, but he rapidly weakened, and at last the cat felt his writhing body go limp beneath her. With a last savage shake, she flung it from her and sank panting to the ground, bleeding from a score of scratches. She felt depressed and exhausted after her gruelling fight with the vicious predator, but she began to feel better when she had washed herself and carefully licked her wounds.

In a little over a fortnight, the cat's scratches were all healed. The weather was still mild; it was as if the earth stood trembling on the brink of winter, afraid to plunge into the bleak and bitter darkness ahead. The leaves of the sycamores beside the clearing turned bright yellow, then fawn and brown, fluttering down in rustling showers to drift against the old bee-hive. Gusts of wind sent them dancing along the river bank, and the cat amused herself by bounding after them, patting them with her fore-paws and tossing them into the air.

In the mornings, the valley was thick with white mist which slowly cleared as the sun rose. The sunsets left a purple glow over the moor and along the river, giving a richer, darker colour to the blackberries which still hung heavy from the brambles and dyeing the haws of the wild rose a deeper crimson.

Then the days began to grow colder, and at night there was sometimes a touch of frost. A small herd of wild ponies, three mares and a stallion, came down from the high moors on their long trek to winter in the low-lands and stopped to graze in the clearing for a few days. For most of the first day they were there, the cat lay high on a sycamore bough, watching them with still, expressionless eyes. She was not afraid of them; she remembered their scent and the sounds they made from the time she had lived in the prison stable, but she was relieved when they moved on. They disturbed the smaller animals and made her hunting more difficult.

A farm-labourer from the village down the valley had heard that there were plenty of rabbits around the clearing, and at the beginning of December he drove up there in his battered old van to trap some of them to raise money for Christmas. He put down a dozen ordinary, wire snares and one cruel, illegal, steel gin, fastening them with strong cord to wooden pegs hammered into the ground. He set the toothed, steel trap in a rabbit-run near the bee-hive, while the cat, lying hidden on a high bough, eyed him suspiciously. She did not know why he had come to the clearing and hammered pieces of wood into the ground, but she instinctively felt that he meant no good.

When the farm-hand had driven off, she scrambled down the tree and warily circled the steel trap he had set near the hive, her whiskers twitching, but she mistrusted it too much to go near it.

Late that night, she heard the thin scream of a rabbit as the serrated jaws of the cruel trap snapped together on its foot. The screaming went on until dawn was near, gradually fading to a whimper as the animal weakened. The man came every day to reset his snares and take the rabbits away in a sack, but the cat still mistrusted him and kept out of his way.

One night, she was stalking a big buck rabbit, slinking noiselessly through the undergrowth, her tail twitching, her stomach brushing the ground. She sprang on to the rabbit's back and started to bury her teeth in his neck to crunch through his spinal cord, but he managed to shake her off and staggered lopsidedly into a patch of long grass. The cat rolled over as she hit the ground, then she heard a sharp, metallic click and felt a searing pain in one of her hind legs. For a moment, the world went black, then through a mist of agony she heard herself screaming.

It was late the next afternoon before the man came to collect his kill. In her frantic struggles to free herself, the cat had managed to pull the peg of the gin out of the ground and had just started to crawl along the river bank, dragging the heavy trap behind her, the fur stripped from her leg and the bone showing through the mangled, bleeding flesh.

The farm-hand raised one of his hobnailed boots to bring it crashing down on the cat's skull, intending to skin her and sell her, but her size saved her; he reluctantly decided that nobody would believe that a wild rabbit could grow that big. The pitiful state of the cat did not worry him in the least, but he wanted to use the gin again, so he prised its teeth apart and set her free. Frantic with pain and fear, she sank her teeth deep in the fleshy part of the labourer's hand. He shook her off and started back, cursing and lashing out at her with his foot, but she rolled out of the way and scrambled off into the undergrowth as fast as her three sound legs would carry her. The man let her go; he did not have much time left to set his traps and he did not want to be out after dark, so near the moor.

For three days and nights, the cat lay on a heap of dried leaves near the river bank, feverish and shivering. Her saliva had dried up, so she could not wash her torn leg, and she had nothing to eat, but she was able to lick a small amount of moisture from the grass around her.

On the fourth day, the fever left her, and she looked around her clear-eyed. She struggled to her feet and found that she could move about on her three sound legs, although the injured one was still stiff, swollen and black with dried blood. She caught and ate a few spiders, which did little to stay her ravenous hunger, and she managed to drag herself down to the water's edge and drink deeply. The water was icy cold, but it strengthened her, and she limped over to the old hive, where she washed her injured leg well before falling into a deep sleep. The torn flesh was slow to knit together again, but she licked it constantly, and gradually the wound healed. She grew lean and hungry; she could not hunt much and had to live as best she could, taking the edge off her hunger with long draughts of water from the river. In the end, she was so hungry that she overcame her fear of the farm-hand's traps and ate part of a rabbit caught in one of them, but the next day he moved on to set his snares in a fresh place, so she was left to fend for herself again.

Fortunately, the first snow did not fall until late in January, and by then the cat was fit and strong again, able to catch birds, mice and an occasional rabbit, sleeping snug and dry in the hive.

Nine

When spring came, the cat went back to Dartmoor, where she mated with an old tom that had gone wild. He was an ugly tabby with torn ears and a battle-scarred face, but he was strong and lusty, and the kittens, born in June, soon after he had travelled on across the moor, were healthy and vigorous. The litter consisted of two females and a male; the little tom a tabby like his father, the other two black, one with a white spot under her chin. Their mother reared them in a nest of bracken on the open moor and took them hunting with her through the summer, but in August the little tom was taken by a fox. The she-cat found his bloodied pelt in a clump of bracken and knew at once what had happened. After that, she kept her two remaining kittens close to her side as they worked their way deeper into the heart of the moor.

It was a hot summer, and everywhere there were countless thousands of insects. Flies swarmed over sheep and other animals that had died, laying eggs in their rotting flesh, and butterflies fluttered from heather tuft to heather tuft. The crimson, leafless stems of dodder with their clusters of reddish flowers were almost hidden by the brightly-coloured wings of orange-tip and common blue butterflies, and the bracken seemed to break into strange blossom when clouds of brown-winged small heath butterflies settled on it.

The cat and her litter caught and ate insects in their hundreds; flies and moths form part of a cat's natural diet, and the kittens grew so good at catching them that they lived almost entirely on them.

One afternoon, the family came across a swarm of flies hovering over a piece of marshy land, and while the she-cat sat washing herself the two youngsters batted down fly after fly, eating the juicy flesh and spitting out the legs and wings. The insects were buzzing round a small plant. Its leaves were fringed with fine, red hairs and grew in the shape of a rosette, and a small white flower on a long, bare stem rose from the centre of the plant. From time to time, a fly, probably attracted by the scent of the sundew, would swoop down and settle on its leaves, then the sticky, red hairs would encircle the insect's body, piercing its flesh and digesting its juices.

The kittens were fascinated, and the one with the white spot stretched out a paw to touch one of the sundew's sticky leaves. The hairs on it clung to her pads, leaving on them a sweet-tasting substance which took her a long time to wash off. Then, tired of catching flies herself, she settled down to watch the carnivorous plant trapping its victims.

The golden afternoon faded into twilight, and the flies began to scatter over the moor. The she-cat, who had stopped washing to doze in the heat of the sun, stretched herself, calling the kittens to her with a soft mewing, and all three of them set off towards a patch of cotton grass from which a faint rustling came. The day was over, and it was time to start hunting in earnest.

October was mild and mellow, and the moor was covered with the delicate silver lace of gossamer spiders' webs, woven on every gorse bush and heather tuft, pearled with dew in the morning sunlight. The heat of the afternoon drew from the earth moisture which gathered in the hollows as patches of mist, and as the month went on and the sun lost heat, the mists grew thicker and often lasted all day long. Sometimes, stray gusts of wind sent swirling, white spirals across the uplands, but most of the time the hills were bathed in sunlight and stood clear and bright above the clouded valleys.

It was good hunting weather; the earth was just damp enough to hold a scent, yet the going was firm, the bogs and mires still dry from summer. The three cats were dozing in the sun one afternoon when their sharp ears caught the distant, hollow thunder of horses' hooves and the faint, spine-chilling music of hounds. The sounds grew steadily louder, and the she-cat knew that the hunt was coming towards them. She started to trot off across the moor, and when the kittens tried to follow her she made them disperse in different directions. She knew nothing about hunts, but she could tell from the wide area covered by the belling of the hounds that, if she and her brood stayed together, all of them would be in danger, while, if they split up and separated, at least one might survive.

One of the kittens ran off down the gravelly bank of a watercourse, the other darted into a thick clump of bracken and their mother bounded over to a granite clitter about fifty yards away. She did not know that the hounds were hot on the scent of a fox, unaware that she and her family existed; instinct told her that she must use all her skill and cunning to lead them away from her kittens. She planned to run out from the rock-pile when the hunt drew near, making sure that the hounds saw her.

Knowing that his scent would not linger long on the granite of the clitter, the wily fox had gone to hide there. He saw the cat coming, and a plan began to take shape in his devious brain. As the cat lay tense and trembling at the base of the rock-pile, waiting for the hunt to come into sight, he ran round and round her in smaller and smaller circles, crossing and recrossing her trail. He ended up passing within inches of her, then he clambered back up the side of the clitter to a ridge high above and ran along it until he came to a granite outcrop and disappeared into a cavern in the rock-face.

The sound of hounds and horses drew nearer and nearer. The cat was terrified, but she knew she must stay and draw the hunt away from her kittens. When the hounds reached the edge of the clitter, they began milling round and round, setting up a frenzied yelping, baffled by the false trail the fox had laid.

The cat broke away from the shelter of the jumbled rocks under their very noses and dashed downhill towards a small stream. The excited hounds saw her at once and took after her in full cry; confused by the mingled scents of fox and cat, they decided that the lithe, black form bounding down the hillside must be their quarry. They poured down after her, an unruly, frantically-yapping rabble, taking no notice of the shouts and curses of the whipper-in.

Desperate with fear, the cat steadily gained on the hounds. Where they ran around granite outcrops, she bounded over them; where they slithered and slid on patches of gravel, she sped lightly over them.

Her strength was beginning to flag, and her breath was coming in great gasps when she reached the stream and crawled into the rushes at the water's edge. Her heart was pounding in her chest, and the blood was throbbing behind her eyes so that she looked out through a red mist, but she knew she had to go on. Threading her way through the thick rushes at the edge of the stream, she headed for a patch of marshy land downstream.

The hounds went streaming down into the valley close behind her, but they lost sight of her when she went into the rushes and scattered in all directions trying to pick up her scent, keeping up a blood-curdling, hysterical yelping.

Then a gust of wind came upstream, driving a wreath of mist before it, and in a few moments the whole valley was filled with the cold, grey, swirling water-vapour. The huntsmen, still high on the hill, were bathed in sunlight, but beneath them the mist lay in a thick blanket, muffling the sound of the hounds and blotting them from sight. The huntsmen reined in their horses at the fringe of the grey sea, afraid to go any further. Below them, there was nothing to be seen but the swirling, grey mist; they felt that one more step might send them plunging over the edge of the world. The Master sounded the recall again and again, and one crestfallen hound after another came slinking out of the damp, grey cloud into the brightness of the sunshine until the whole pack had turned up, subdued and frightened. To be caught in a Dartmoor mist is an alarming experience for animals and men alike.

The cat lay trembling in a patch of reed mace on the piece of marshy land. Hounds had blundered within a few feet of her as they tried to find her, but the grey cloud had hidden her from them, and the heavy moisture content of the air had masked her scent.

As soon as she had regained her breath, she set off downstream, picking her way along the water's edge, pausing from time to time to cast a wary glance backwards, but behind her the mist lay still and silent.

She walked and ran until her pads were sore and her legs ached, then the grey of the mist gave way to the blackness of a moonless night. She had reached the foothills of the moor, but still she did not feel safe. Fear of the yelping hounds still lay at the back of her mind, and she limped on and on until she dropped, exhausted, and slept where she lay.

Next day, she headed east, travelling as fast as she could, only stopping to hunt food or to drink from the widening stream. She was so terrified that she had forgotten the kittens she had left on the moor; her only thought was to put as much distance as possible between herself and the place where she had so narrowly escaped being torn to pieces by the slavering, yelping hounds.

A few days later, she had left the moor behind and was going through the rich, red land of mid-Devon. The red mud clung to her paws and splattered her coat, and she found the going much harder than the gravelly surface of the moor, but slowly she began to realise that she was safe. She listened, and all was still, but instead of the ringing silence of Dartmoor there was an undertone of movement, a hum of life, the distant sound of traffic on the main roads.

Ten

The cat spent that winter in a tumbledown barn on an isolated farm, warm and dry, living well on the rats and mice that infested the old building, then when spring came she slowly carried on across country. Although her long trek down from the moor had been broken by her winter's rest in the barn, it had sapped her strength. She was beginning to feel old and tired, but she was determined to go on; nowhere did she see a place where she wanted to settle down.

She came to the outskirts of the town where she was born, but she did not recognise it; she no longer remembered the scents and sounds she had known as a kitten. More and more she wanted to find a place where she could rest from her wanderings, and in her heart there was a deep longing for kindness and affection and the company of men; she remembered the warmth and security of the prison stables and the kindness and understanding of the watchman at the clay-pits.

Spring began to give way to summer, and the nights were heavy with the scent of wild roses and honeysuckle. The fields were green with growing corn in which it was very difficult to hunt, and although the cat managed to kill enough to stay alive, she felt more and more frightened and alone.

It was late in June when she found the cottage, a small stone and thatch building set back from the road behind an unkempt lawn with an elder tree in blossom. A lean-to wooden shed buttressed one end wall, and there, among the stacked logs and kindling, she slept the whole of that afternoon. When evening came, she woke and from her hiding-place saw a man come out of the cottage and sit smoking on a bench under the elder tree. He was old and grey and moved slowly, and there was an air of tranquillity and kindness about him. The cat knew that her wanderings were over. She had found the home she needed.

She made no move towards the man for a few days. She was still sleeping in the wood-shed, killing mice for food and going down the field behind the cottage to drink at the stream running through it. Every evening, the old man came out to smoke his last pipe on the seat under the tree, and once an elderly woman sat there and watched the sunset with him. The cat crouched on a pile of logs, her eyes half-hooded, watching them until they went back into the cottage in the gathering darkness.

One evening, when the man was sitting on the bench alone, she crept out of the shed and rubbed herself against his legs. He showed no surprise; he bent down and ran his hand along the length of the cat's back and then went on smoking as if nothing had happened. His movements were gentle and unhurried.

After that, the cat often went out to him when he sat under the elder, sometimes purring round his legs, sometimes sitting aloof, washing herself and eyeing him speculatively. One day, the old man called for his wife to bring a saucer of milk and some scraps "for the stray", but the cat was nervous of the woman and would not eat or drink when she was there, nor would she go into the cottage, although the old couple did their best to persuade her to.

A vet who lived near the cottage told the old people that, in his opinion, she was a feral cat, a domestic animal that had gone wild. He did not think she would ever become fully domesticated again and advised the old couple to let her go on living in the wood-shed, taking, perhaps stealing, what food she wanted, and to gain her confidence by giving her constant, undemanding affection. He told them that the cat might go as suddenly as she had come, and that she was still essentially a wild animal which could turn vicious for little reason. She would be wayward, uncertain and suspicious, demanding affection but giving little in return, he told the elderly couple, but she would keep the place free of mice and would be scrupulously clean. He hinted that it might be better to have the cat put down, because neither domestic life nor living wild would agree with her, and she would grow more and more unhappy as she grew older.

The old people would not hear of having her put down; already they were used to having her around the place, and the old man felt sure that in the end they would be able to persuade her to live in the cottage with them.

Towards the end of August, the flower beds in the cottage garden were aglow with asters and chrysanthemums. The creamy pads of blossom on the elder tree had long since fallen, and the green berries that had followed them were darkening to purple and black. The evenings were growing cooler, and the sun was setting earlier, but the old man still sat on the bench under the tree to smoke his last pipe of the day. He always took out some milk for the cat, and some more milk and some scraps were left just inside the cottage door, but no matter how tempting the scent of the food was, the cat would not go into the strange-smelling building for it. The old people put down raw liver, fish and shredded beef, but although she would stalk over and look in through the open door, she would not go inside the cottage. It was very different from the few buildings she had known since she had gone wild; it smelt of humans, of disinfectant, of stale food and tobacco smoke. She felt a deep, instinctive fear that, once she had crossed the threshold, the door would clang to behind her and she would never be let out again. In any case, she could manage without the food they put down for her; the mice in the shed, the birds and the fat bluebottles in the garden were enough for her.

The elder berries had grown so fat and black and juicy that they were beginning to fall from the tree, so the old man and his wife took out baskets to fill with the fruit. The cat hovered round them as they worked, pouncing on any berries that fell out of the baskets, trying to toss them between her paws. When the baskets were full, the man took them into the house and came back with a rabbit's paw tied on a piece of string. He dangled it in front of the cat, and she went nearly wild with excitement, batting it with her forepaws and trying to seize it in her teeth, but the old man kept pulling it out of her reach. He went to sit on the seat under the tree, and the cat followed him and sat on the grass near him, looking up at him, mewing impatiently for the game to start again. The man took the rabbit's paw out of his pocket and slowly drew it towards him along the bench. The cat eagerly sprang up after it, and the old man let her pounce on it and claw it. He then drew it slowly along the seat, and the cat went with it, finishing up lying beside him with her head resting against his thigh, purring her pleasure.

When the evenings drew in and grew too cold for the man to sit under the elder tree, he left the cottage door ajar while he had the last smoke of the day in his easy chair by the fire. The cat missed him and prowled restlessly from the bench to the cottage door and back again, mewing plaintively. The old man could see the green gleam of her eyes and the dark bulk of her body silhouetted against the fading light, but she would not go into the house.

Autumn faded into winter, and the first frosts made the garden paths crisp beneath the fallen leaves which littered them. Beside the wood-shed, a giant sunflower hung its bedraggled head, and a pink hydrangea in a tub by the front door of the cottage faded to a dingy fawn. The cat was still sleeping in the shed, living mainly on the mice she caught but taking the scraps and milk the old couple left outside the cottage door for her. She rarely saw them since the wintry weather had come; when the man went to fetch logs in the day, she was usually asleep, and it was too cold for them to leave the cottage door ajar in the evening. The floor of the wood-shed was littered with the tails of the mice she had caught, but as winter went on the mice grew fewer and fewer. She was slowly wiping them out.

December was unusually cold, and there was a heavy fall of snow. The cottage was cut off by thigh-deep drifts, but the old people had plenty of food, and the man cleared a path to the shed so he could fetch logs when they were needed. He saw no sign of the cat when he went out there, and the milk and scraps were left untouched outside the cottage door. He began to think that she had gone away, as the vet had said she might.

The day before Christmas, when he went out for a basket of logs, the cat suddenly appeared at his feet, and when he went back with the wood she followed him in through the open door. She ran straight to the hearth-rug as if she had lived in the cottage all her life, and after a few exploratory sniffs she curled up and went to sleep, her fur steaming in the heat of the fire. The man and his wife were shocked at the state she was in; she was so thin that her ribs and hip-bones stood out under her sagging skin, but they thought it wiser not to wake her up to give her food. When they went to bed, they banked the fire with ash and put canned fish and milk in saucers on the kitchen floor, leaving the cat still sleeping soundly, curled up head-to-tail on the rug.

Next morning, there was no sign of her, and the fish and milk stood untouched in the kitchen, but some scraps left in a tidy by the sink had been eaten, and later they found the cat hiding under the couch in the living-room. They took no notice of her and went about their business as if they had not seen her, then after a while she crept out from her hiding-place and started to wash herself on the hearth-rug.

When the front door was opened, she ran out into the garden, but she came back a few minutes later and crawled under the couch again. The old people realised that she was very nervous and had only been driven into the cottage by hunger and cold. They remembered that the vet had said that she would perhaps prefer to steal what food she wanted, so they left some scraps of beef on the draining-board when they went to bed. In the morning, all the meat was eaten.

The cold spell went on for several weeks, but no more snow fell. The cat still spent most of the day hiding under the couch, but sometimes she came out, and in the evening she always lay on the hearth-rug watching the old people reading or sewing. At night, she prowled round the house looking for food, either catching mice or "stealing" the scraps and milk left for her on the draining-board.

When the warmer weather came, she did not go back to the wood-shed. She had gradually grown less nervous and suspicious and had begun to eat from a plate put on the floor under the sink which she had adopted as her feeding-place. She nearly always slept in front of the fire during the day, but she was still uncertain and suspicious, sometimes purring and rubbing herself against the old people's legs, sometimes scurrying away from them to crawl under the couch or one of the easy chairs, watching them from her hiding-place with nervous, fear-brightened eyes.

Eleven

In March, when the wind blew soft from the western ocean and the warm rains had washed the last traces of frost from the rich, red earth, the old man started to plant his early potatoes in the garden patch behind the cottage. The cat sat on the path washing herself as she watched him work, pausing from time to time to eye him contemplatively as if making sure he was doing the job properly. Every time he saw her looking at him, the man spoke to her, talking about the weather, the stickiness of the soil, the crop he hoped to raise, and anything else that entered his head, whether it made sense or not. Although she did not understand a word he said, the sound of his voice filled the cat with a deep contentment until her happiness, heightened by the soft warmth of the sun and the feeling of spring in the air, grew almost unbearable. She could not stay still and padded over to the old man, circling his legs, tail up and purring. Her excitement and affection encouraged him to do something he had never done before. He picked her up and cradled her in his arms. At first, she was afraid and struggled to break free, but after a minute or so she lay still, purring loudly. From then on, whenever the man sat in his easy chair by the fireside or on the bench under the elder tree, she would curl up on his lap, her contented purring showing the understanding and trust between them. The cat tolerated the woman's petting and would even roll over on the rug and present her stomach to be tickled, but she would never sit on her lap, nor would she let the woman pick her up, and sometimes the cat still withdrew from both the old people and sprang up on to the window-sill, where she sat staring with expressionless eyes into the distance.

The next time the vet came to the cottage, he was surprised to see how affectionate the cat had grown. He told the old couple that it was very unusual for a cat that had lived wild to allow people to fondle it. Most feral cats, he said, were vicious and untamable; he had felt sure that the she-cat would have moved on long before, leaving his friends relieved to see the back of her.

The cat was sleeping peacefully on the hearth-rug, occasionally opening an eye to see what the old man was doing as he sat smoking in his chair beside the fire. She woke and rolled from side to side under the gentle pressure of the woman's foot and let the vet stroke her. He asked what name they had given her, and the old man told him that they just called her "the cat" or "the stray".

The vet went to the cottage again towards the end of May, and he and the old man were sitting on the bench under the tree when a terrified squeaking broke out in the wood-shed. The cat came out carrying a half-dead mouse in her mouth and put it down on the grass near the old man, batting it from side to side with her fore-paws. One of its legs was broken, and it could only drag itself along the ground an inch or two at a time as it tried to escape. The old man ended its suffering by grinding it into the ground with his heel and flung its body over the hedge into the road.

The cat, bursting with pride, went to rub herself against his legs, but he took no notice and puffed angrily on his pipe. The vet asked him why he was annoyed; after all, it was a cat's nature to hunt mice, and cruelty, as we know it, did not exist among animals, he said. To be cruel, it was necessary to imagine and understand another's pain, and this no animal could do, he told the old man. To a cat, a mouse was something to be pounced on and killed as quickly or as slowly as appetite, or lack of appetite, dictated. Its agility and cunning were merely tests of its hunter's skill, a way of keeping a cat's muscles supple, its brain alert and its eyes keen. If the old man wanted his cat to kill swiftly and cleanly, his friend went on, he would have to starve her. The old man said nothing, but a minute or two later he reached down and ran his hand along the cat's back.

The shadows lengthened, and dusk began to fall. In a hazel tree across the road, a bird began to sing, and the land seemed to fall silent under the shivering sweetness of its music. First, three or four notes were repeated several times with a pause in between, then the bird burst into full song, and the two men were held spellbound by the incredible cascade of sound. The notes came clear and true, one after the other, rising to a crescendo in which one note of unutterable sweetness was held for what seemed like an age. The song pulsed and vibrated against the hushed stillness of the night, finally trilling away into silence, then one clear note was repeated at regular intervals, after which came again the snatch of liquid song the bird had started with.

There was a rustling sound in the hazel tree, and a small bird stood out in jerky flight against the rising moon. The vet pointed to it, but both men kept silent, still enthralled by the magic of the nightingale's song. Even the cat seemed stunned by it, lying stretched out with her head on her forepaws, but before long the thousand noises of the night broke the silence again. Sparrows twittered in the eaves of the cottage, a cow lowed in the distance, an owl hooted, a dog barked. Slowly, the world came back to life again.

The old man puffed thoughtfully at his pipe. A cat had tortured a mouse with savage cruelty, then an insignificant-looking little bird had cast a spell over every living thing that had heard the unearthly sweetness of its song.

No longer forced to hunt for her food, the cat was putting on weight, and as her frame filled out and her fur grew thick and glossy, she began to feel restless. Sometimes, the west wind carried the faint scent of heather and gorse, and she began to long for the space and freedom of the moor. Night after night, she stayed out, ranging the garden and the fields, and in the day she took to sleeping in the double hedge behind the cottage. The old couple watched her anxiously, but the man said that if she wanted to leave she must be allowed to; it would be cruel to try to stop her.

In July, there was a spell of humid heat which lay suffocatingly on the land. The cat lay listless in the garden, only leaving the shade of the elder tree to eat and drink. Day after day, the heat built up until late one evening a flash of lightning flickered across the distant outline of the moor, throwing the jagged outline of the tors into sharp relief, and a cool breeze whispered across the lowlands. The cat was suddenly full of energy, dashing aimlessly up and down the garden path and in and out of the cottage in the gathering dusk. The old people watched her from the bench under the tree. The man laughed and called to her, and she bounded over to him, her fur on end, her eyes glowing emerald with excitement, but after batting his trouser-legs with her paws and springing on his lap and off again, she dashed off. When night fell, she would not go into the cottage. Ignoring the old couple's calls, she ran off into the darkness.

The storm hit the lowlands soon after midnight. The lightning was so bright that it woke the old man up, and he went to the bedroom window to watch. The first drops of rain bounced like tiny balls from the thick dust in the road, then, with blinding flashes of lightning and ear-splitting claps of thunder, it began to lash down with savage fury. The old man saw the cat sitting by the garden gate with her face turned towards the moor, her wet fur plastered to her, her head stretched out, her ears pricked as she listened intently.

Next morning, she was nowhere to be found, and the old people sadly decided that they would probably never see her again. The storm had aroused disturbing emotions in the cat. For some time, life at the cottage had seemed dull and pointless, but her affection for the old man had stopped her going away. Regular food and easy living had given her back her strength, and she had gradually felt more and more like striking out on her own again. Life in the small world of the cottage, the garden and the fields around had grown boringly safe and uneventful. On the night of the storm, the lashing downpour had brought with it the scent of the bogs and mires whose waters the sun had sucked up to make the rain-clouds. Suddenly, she had felt that she had to go.

She trudged across the sodden fields until her fur was yellow with the pollen of buttercups and her paws were caked with red mud. She walked without stopping until her shadow shrank in the noonday sun to a puddle of darkness directly beneath her. Only then did she pause to wash and to find food.

Late in the afternoon, she resumed her westward trek. Already the dark outline of Dartmoor loomed much nearer, and the hot, sweet scent of gorse was in her nostrils. The going grew easier as she neared the foot-hills of the moor; the wet, red clay gave way to well-drained gravel, the lush grass and meadow flowers grew less thick on the land. She had headed straight for the moor, ignoring roads and cart-tracks, scrambling over hedges, leaping over or wading through the streams which barred her way, shortening the journey by miles.

By midnight, she had come to a stretch of high common land bordered by a patchwork of cultivated fields, faintly visible in the light of the moon. She slept where she dropped, exhausted.

She woke as dawn was breaking and hunted and killed until her hunger was satisfied, then she sat in a clump of heather washing herself, preparing to leave life as a house-cat behind for ever, to go down the valley and up the other side to the moor from which she would never return.

Strangely, she was loath to start. As the sun climbed higher in the sky, the heady scents of the open moorland filled her nostrils, but suddenly they no longer beckoned her on. She sat as if in a trance, her forelegs close together, her tail neatly curled, her head and neck stretched out as she stared across the valley, snuffing the crisp morning air, ignoring the young blackbird hopping within inches of her, deaf to the dawn chorus rising around her. Dim memories of her life on the moor flitted through her mind with the muddled inconsequence of a dream, and with them came the smell of fear and starvation, the acrid reek of burning heather. She sighed and stood up, turning her back on the moor and heading eastwards.

Twelve

It was nearly a month later when the cat turned up at the cottage, dusty, footsore and weary. The old man and his wife were delighted to see her again, but she was listless and withdrawn, eating without interest the food they gave her and accepting their petting indifferently. The wood-shed was infested with mice again, but she did not seem to care; although she sometimes killed one or two of them and took their tails to the cottage door, she did it as if it was the most boring, pointless job imaginable.

The smell of mice in the shed grew so strong that a yellow, neutered tom from one of the cottages along the road took to prowling round outside the garden. The she-cat eyed him balefully but did nothing, then one evening he slunk in through the open gate and, watching her warily, stalked towards the wood-shed. For a moment or two, the she-cat stood stiff-legged and tense, the fur on her back and neck standing on end, then she swore softly at the other cat and suddenly launched herself at him. All the resentment and frustration of the last few weeks boiled up in her as she pounced on the scentless intruder, the non-cat that had dared to trespass on her territory, her claws raking his back, her teeth sinking into his shoulder. For a while, he stood his ground, but the fury of the she-cat's attack soon knocked the fight out of him. Howling dismally, he managed to shake her off and made a frantic dash for the road. The she-cat darted after him, spitting taunts and threats as he disappeared into the gathering darkness.

The old man had been watching the fight from the cottage window and saw the cat's eyes glowing green as she came back, stalking stiff-legged and triumphant up the path. He realised that at last she had accepted the cottage and garden as her home, a home she was ready to fight for.

From then on, the cat's attitude towards the old people changed. Wherever the man went, she followed, rubbing herself against his legs and purring when he bent down to stroke her. In the evenings, she sat on his lap, her liquid eyes big with affection, kneading his knees with her paws until the sharpness of her slightly-spread claws grew unbearable and he had to put her down on the floor. She clung to the woman's skirts, teasing her until she rolled her over with her foot and tickled her stomach, making her purr so loudly that her whole body pulsed and vibrated. She took to sleeping at the foot of the old couple's bed, moulding herself round their feet, waking when they did and watching with affection and concern every movement they made.

After Christmas, the old woman fell ill, and her husband spent most of each day sitting at her bedside with the cat on his lap. Sensing that the man was worried, she sat still and quiet and did not try to jump on to the bed because she knew it would upset her mistress.

Then came a day when the cat sensed that the man was no longer sad and anxious and she knew that the woman was feeling better. The cat went pirouetting round and round the room in a wild dance of joy, leaping on and off the furniture, rolling and tumbling over and over on the floor. The old man laughed for the first time since his wife had been ill, and even the sick woman had to smile. The more the man laughed, the more boisterous the cat's antics grew, until she collapsed, exhausted, at his feet.

The woman gradually regained her strength, and the three of them were able to potter round the cottage and garden again, but the old couple could see that the cat was beginning to age. Her coat was drab and rusty, she often felt twinges of rheumatism in her hips and she walked stiffly when the weather was cold or damp.

When spring came, the blood no longer sang in her veins, and the scent of lilac and hyacinths no longer filled her with a heady excitement which made her long to go off and leave the monotony of life at the cottage far behind her. She spent most of her nights sleeping on the hearth-rug and during the day she padded slowly round the garden, soberly content.

Summer started early with a heat-wave in May, and

the hot weather went on without a break until August. The long, slow days were drenched with sun from dawn till dusk, and the red soil was baked to a pale pink. The cat spent most of the hot, lazy days stretched out on the lawn at the edge of the shade cast by the elder tree, feeling the heat of the sun soaking into her bones, easing her aches and pains and bringing back some of the suppleness to her joints. Before going into the cottage for her supper, she would sharpen her claws on the trunk of the tree, stretching and pulling until the muscles of her back and thighs moved freely and smoothly. Sometimes, she would try to persuade the old man to play with her, but he would laugh and tell her that she was too old to behave like a kitten, picking her up and stroking her until she lay dozing in sleepy contentment on his lap.

When autumn came, the nights were heavy with dew, and the cat stayed indoors until the heat of the sun had sucked up the damp from the earth, but she always spent the afternoons in the garden, savouring the crisp, rich autumnal smells and sometimes playing with the golden leaves that drifted down from the elder tree.

In the evening, dozing on the hearth-rug or curled up on the old man's lap, she was filled with happiness and a timeless sense of well-being. It was as if she had always been warm and well-fed, as if she had never known the hardship and danger of life on the moor, never been lonely or frightened or in pain.

One day in November, the wind blew strong from the north, and the elder was stripped of its few remaining leaves. The weather was crisp and cold, and the feel of coming winter was in the air. The boisterous wind excited the cat, and all that morning she was unusually playful.

Later in the day, she trotted through the open gate on to the road, trying to catch a drift of leaves dancing along before the wind. The old man, working in the garden, heard the impatient sound of a horn and the squeal of brakes. He looked up and saw the cat tossed high into the air. The car picked up speed and went on. It was only a cat.

The old man hurried out to her and found her lying on the grass verge at the edge of the road. She was still conscious, and her eyes turned pleadingly to him, but he could see that she was badly injured. Her hind legs were useless, and a thin trickle of blood was oozing from her mouth and spreading over the white of her bib.

He took off his jacket and gently lifted her on to it. She winced when he touched her, but her eyes were filled with love and trust as he carefully carried her into the cottage, using the jacket as a sling. He made her as comfortable as he could on the hearth-rug and ran down the road to fetch the vet.

When the two friends came hurrying back, the cat was still alive, gasping and trembling on the rug. The woman had washed the blood from the cat's mouth and was crouching beside her, gently stroking her head and murmuring endearments to her.

The vet told the old people that the cat had internal injuries as well as a broken back, and the only possible thing he could do was to end her suffering. The old man nodded; he had known all the time, but he had hoped against hope. The cat's eyes already had a strange, faraway look; it was as if she was looking back into the past, he thought.

The vet opened his bag and took out a syringe which he carefully filled. The woman turned away, but her husband gently stroked the cat's head and spoke soothingly to her as the needle plunged into her thigh. She twitched once, then she sighed as all her pain went from her. Her head fell forward, a trickle of saliva dribbled from her lips, and then her body went limp as she drifted away to that far-off land where there is everlasting peace.

STAY ON

Here are details of other exciting TARGET titles. If you cannot obtain these books from your local bookshop, or newsagent, write to the address below listing the titles you would like and enclosing cheque or postal order—*not* currency—including 7p per book to cover packing and postage; 2–4 books, 5p per copy; 5–8 books, 4p per copy.

TARGET BOOKS,
Universal-Tandem Publishing Co.,
14 Gloucester Road,
London SW7 4RD

WELL MET BY WITCHLIGHT   30p
Nina Beachcroft
0 426 10356 4   **A Target Adventure**
In which Sarah, Christopher and Lucy meet a strange little old woman called Mary, a 'white' witch who can tame animals, raise wind and water, change her shape and, yes—actually fly on a broomstick! Whether or not she can deal with the evil-eyed Mrs Bella Black, a very powerful 'black' witch who lives in the next village, is another matter which concerns the children very much as they are caught up into the middle of a terrifyingly dangerous battle fought out between the two witches on the supernatural plane.

THE HUMBLES
Hilary Seton

0 426 10698 9

THE HUMBLES are a family of little people living in, or, as they would say, caretaking for, a huge old house in the country. Aunt Tilly Humble's pies are the best ever, and Grandfather Ganderglas' tomatoes the pride of the district. But when Araminta Humble hears about THE MINDERS, those people who look after things, she knows the time has come for her family to leave their beautiful home and make a journey . . . over the hills and far away . . . to the village where The Minders live. *Illustrated.*

30p

THE 2nd TARGET BOOK OF FUN AND GAMES
Nicola Davies

0 426 10532 X

A further book of fun and games to tease and test your wits: jokes; riddles; tongue-twisters; mazes; experiments; funny poems; picture-puzzles; tricks; cartoons; and never a dull moment!

30p

THE LONDON QUIZ BOOK
R. W. Wilson

0 426 10436 6

Going on a day visit or holiday to London? Have fun by asking your friends, and yourself for that matter, questions about this most exciting of all the capital cities in the world! Questions on: Royal London; Government; Law and Order; museums; the Thames; zoos and parks; statues; famous buildings; ancient traditions and so forth . . . *Illustrated.*

30p

THAT MAD, BAD BADGER
Molly Burkett

0 426 10399 4

A blow-by-blow true account of life with 'Nikki' the badger, who delights in whipping laces out of the shoes of unsuspecting visitors to the Burkett household, stealing goodies from the 'fridge, and lying tummyside-up in a comfortable armchair for a quiet snooze. There have been other stories about badgers, but never one like this! *Illustrated.*

25p

BADJELLY THE WITCH   60p
Spike Milligan
0 426 10567 2

ROSE, who is five, and TIM, who is six, go into the forest to
look for LUCY the cow, who is lost. There they meet
MUDWIGGLE the worm, and DINGLEMOUSE the
mouse who is really a banana, BINKLE-BONK the tree
goblin (they sleep in his tree), and, worst of all, BADJELLY
THE WICKEDEST WITCH IN ALL THE WORLD
WHO TURNS CHILDREN INTO SAUSAGES AND
EATS THEM. *A fairy story. Illustrated.*

FAMOUS HISTORICAL MYSTERIES   35p
Leonard Gribble
0 426 10428 5

Ten of the most famous and intriguing mysteries in inter-
national history, many of them still unsolved today. Try and
discover the truth beneath the facts and fallacies which
surround, among others: Anastasia, Princess of Russia; The
Dreyfus Case; the disappearance of Amelia Earhart; the
Mary Celeste, ghost-ship; and the secret identity of the Prisoner
in the Iron Mask . . . *Illustrated.*

HAUNTED HOUSES   30p
Bernhardt J. Hurwood
0 426 10559 1   **A Target Mystery**

Who was the ghost of Powis Castle? Why has he not been
seen for 200 years? What was the cause of the fatal curse on
Mouse Tower? And why does Anne Boleyn ride headless with
a coach and four around the grounds of Blicking Hall? Here
are 25 spine-chilling tales to spirit you away . . . into HAUNTED
HOUSES! *Illustrated.*

SEA-GREEN MAGIC   30p
Elisabeth Beresford
0 426 10479 x   **A Target Adventure**

In which Johnny finds a funny, square-shaped bottle with a
strange misty look about it whilst exploring sea-side rock
pools. Imprisoned inside is an Arabian Djinn, or genie, who
when released is destined to create some awkward problems
for Johnny, Lorna and Alan. *Illustrated.*

If you enjoyed this book and would like to have information sent you about other TARGET titles, write to the address below.

You will also receive:
A FREE TARGET BADGE!
Based on the TARGET BOOKS symbol—see front cover of this book—this attractive three-colour badge, pinned to your blazer-lapel or jumper, will excite the interest and comment of all your friends!

and you will be further entitled to:
FREE ENTRY INTO THE TARGET DRAW!
All you have to do is cut off the coupon beneath, write on it your name and address in *block capitals*, and pin it to your letter. Twice a year, in June and December, coupons will be drawn 'from the hat' and the winner will receive a complete year's set of TARGET books.

Write to:

TARGET BOOKS,
Universal-Tandem
Publishing Co.
14, Gloucester Road,
London SW7 4RD

If you live in South Africa, write to:

TARGET BOOKS,
Purnell & Sons,
505, C.N.A. Building,
110, Commissioner Street,
Johannesburg

If you live in New Zealand, write to:

TARGET BOOKS,
Whitcoulls Ltd.,
111, Cashel Street,
Christchurch

If you live in Australia, write to:

TARGET BOOKS,
Rical Enterprises Pty. Ltd.,
Daking House,
11, Rawson Place,
Sydney, N.S. Wales 2000

———————————— cut here ————————————

Full name..

Address..

....

....

Age...................................

PLEASE ENCLOSE A SELF-ADDRESSED ENVELOPE WITH YOUR COUPON.